FROM THE NANCY DREW FILES

THE CASE: *Sabotage puts skater Yoko Hamara in the hospital—and puts a multimillion-dollar piece of computer hardware into the hands of a smuggler!*

CONTACT: *George's boyfriend, Kevin Davis, is on hand to cover the skating championship—a competition in which crime is the main event.*

SUSPECTS: Brian Adderly—*Yoko's coach is determined to keep his job and has threatened to end her career if she fires him.*

Veronica Taylor—*A former national champion, she stands to lose prestige and money if Yoko comes out on top.*

Trish O'Connell—*The daughter of the scoreboard's owner, she alone among the skaters knew the precise location of the computer chips.*

COMPLICATION: *Has Kevin Davis told Nancy everything he knows? George isn't about to trust him—especially when she discovers him in Veronica's arms!*

Books in The Nancy Drew Files® Series

#1 SECRETS CAN KILL
#2 DEADLY INTENT
#3 MURDER ON ICE
#4 SMILE AND SAY MURDER
#5 HIT AND RUN HOLIDAY
#6 WHITE WATER TERROR
#7 DEADLY DOUBLES
#8 TWO POINTS TO MURDER
#9 FALSE MOVES
#10 BURIED SECRETS
#11 HEART OF DANGER
#12 FATAL RANSOM
#13 WINGS OF FEAR
#14 THIS SIDE OF EVIL
#15 TRIAL BY FIRE
#16 NEVER SAY DIE
#17 STAY TUNED FOR DANGER
#18 CIRCLE OF EVIL
#19 SISTERS IN CRIME
#20 VERY DEADLY YOURS
#21 RECIPE FOR MURDER
#22 FATAL ATTRACTION
#23 SINISTER PARADISE
#24 TILL DEATH DO US PART
#25 RICH AND DANGEROUS
#26 PLAYING WITH FIRE
#27 MOST LIKELY TO DIE
#28 THE BLACK WIDOW
#29 PURE POISON
#30 DEATH BY DESIGN
#31 TROUBLE IN TAHITI
#32 HIGH MARKS FOR MALICE
#33 DANGER IN DISGUISE
#34 VANISHING ACT
#35 BAD MEDICINE
#36 OVER THE EDGE
#37 LAST DANCE
#38 THE FINAL SCENE
#39 THE SUSPECT NEXT DOOR
#40 SHADOW OF A DOUBT
#41 SOMETHING TO HIDE
#42 THE WRONG CHEMISTRY
#43 FALSE IMPRESSIONS
#44 SCENT OF DANGER
#45 OUT OF BOUNDS
#46 WIN, PLACE OR DIE
#47 FLIRTING WITH DANGER
#48 A DATE WITH DECEPTION
#49 PORTRAIT IN CRIME
#50 DEEP SECRETS
#51 A MODEL CRIME
#52 DANGER FOR HIRE
#53 TRAIL OF LIES
#54 COLD AS ICE
#55 DON'T LOOK TWICE
#56 MAKE NO MISTAKE
#57 INTO THIN AIR
#58 HOT PURSUIT
#59 HIGH RISK
#60 POISON PEN
#61 SWEET REVENGE
#62 EASY MARKS
#63 MIXED SIGNALS
#64 THE WRONG TRACK
#65 FINAL NOTES
#66 TALL, DARK AND DEADLY
#67 NOBODY'S BUSINESS
#68 CROSSCURRENTS
#69 RUNNING SCARED
#70 CUTTING EDGE

Available from ARCHWAY Paperbacks

THE NANCY DREW FILES™

Case 70

CUTTING EDGE

CAROLYN KEENE

AN ARCHWAY PAPERBACK
Published by POCKET BOOKS
New York London Toronto Sydney Tokyo Singapore

This book is a work of fiction. Names, characters, places, and incidents are either the product of the author's imagination or are used fictitiously. Any resemblance to actual events or locales or persons, living or dead, is entirely coincidental.

AN ARCHWAY PAPERBACK *Original*

An Archway Paperback published by
POCKET BOOKS, a division of Simon & Schuster Inc.
1230 Avenue of the Americas, New York, NY 10020

Produced by Mega-Books of New York, Inc.

ISBN: 0-671-73074-6

First Archway Paperback printing April 1992

10 9 8 7 6 5 4 3 2 1

Cover art by Tricia Zimic

Printed in the U.S.A.

IL 6+

Chapter One

"WASN'T IT SWEET of Kevin to invite us to the ice-skating championships?" George Fayne said with a sigh.

Nancy Drew was struck once again by the dreamy look in George's brown eyes. Ever since George had met sports announcer Kevin Davis, that soft expression was becoming permanent.

No wonder, Nancy thought. George and Kevin had a lot in common. They were both crazy about sports. George was a serious tennis player, bicyclist, and marathoner. As for Kevin, he'd once been a silver medal decathlon winner at the Olympics.

The two had met when George was in Chicago

to run the Heartland Marathon, which Kevin was covering. The marathon had turned into a race with danger in a case Nancy called *Running Scared,* but one good thing had come of it—George and Kevin had started dating.

"It *was* nice of him," Nancy agreed, pulling her blue Mustang into the parking lot of the Montgomery Sports Arena, which was located on the outskirts of Chicago. She took a ticket from the attendant and pulled into the first free parking space. "I love ice-skating. Great skaters make it seem so easy," she said to George.

"Which it definitely is *not,*" George insisted. "Every time I try figure skating, I feel like a total klutz."

"Come on, George," Nancy said as she turned off the engine. "You're such a good speed skater—I'm sure if you'd practiced—"

"And practiced and practiced," George said, laughing. "You can't believe how dedicated figure skaters are, Nan. They spend so much time on the ice that they hardly have personal lives."

Nancy stepped out into the crisp autumn air, shook out her reddish blond hair, and slipped on an angora beret that matched her blue eyes perfectly. Kevin had warned her and George that the rink would be chilly, especially the day before the crowds arrived.

"Look, the Worldwide Sports truck!" George said with a bright smile. She pointed across the lot to a silver van with a logo of a globe. A young man with broad shoulders and light brown hair was just stepping out of the side of the truck. He was wearing black jeans and a heavy heather gray turtleneck.

"There's Kevin," George said excitedly. Running a hand through her short, dark brown hair, she glanced at her reflection in the car window. "Does my hair look okay?" she asked. She tugged on her olive green cable-knit sweater. "What about this sweater? Does it make me look fat?"

Nancy laughed at her friend. "You look great, George," she assured her. "Let's go say hi."

The two friends hurried across the parking lot to the Worldwide truck.

Kevin's hazel eyes sparkled when he saw the girls. Holding out his arms, he enveloped George in a big hug, then gave her a lingering kiss.

"Hi, Nancy," Kevin said, smiling at her after he and George pulled apart. "Have you two been inside yet?"

"We just got here," Nancy explained.

"I came out to help Mike with some cables," Kevin told them. "Good timing."

The door of the van slid open again, and a slender dark-haired young man appeared, wearing a plaid shirt and jeans. In his hands was a tangle of heavy orange cable. "This should do it, Kev," he said. When he noticed Nancy and George, he broke into a grin. "Friends of yours?"

"Mike, I'd like you to meet my girlfriend, George Fayne, and her friend Nancy Drew," Kevin said, catching the cable Mike tossed him. "Mike Campo is with our crew," he explained to the girls. "Come on. We'd better head back inside. We'll go around the side, where the crew is loading in."

Walking around the neatly landscaped brick arena, Nancy realized it was even larger than it had appeared from the highway. The main section of the long, low building had a huge curved dome for a roof. At the far end of the dome, two wings branched out from the main building. "Wow," Nancy said, letting out a whistle. "This place is enormous!

"It's the biggest sports complex in this part of the world, that's for sure," Kevin said with a laugh. "It's easy to get lost once you're inside, too, believe me!"

"The main rink is under the dome," Mike explained as they headed around the arena. "The complex is built in a giant Y shape. The branch over there, on the far side, has a restaurant, training center, and administrative offices. You can't see it from here."

"There's a whole underground level, too, where the dressing rooms are," Kevin added.

At the loading dock a sign next to the double doors read "American Skating Federation—Staff and Crew Only." A uniformed guard stood beside it.

"Oops," George said when she saw the guard. "Nancy and I had better go around front."

"No problem. You're with me, and I'm a very important guy. Or didn't you realize that?" Kevin joked, laying his arm on her shoulder. He nodded to the guard. "These ladies are with me. I'm taking them in to get their passes now."

The guard nodded back. "Okay, Mr. Davis."

"Mr. Davis, huh?" George said, a twinkle in her eye. "I guess you *are* pretty important."

Kevin replied with a grin, "And don't you forget it!"

Nancy's eyes widened when she stepped through the corridor and into the arena. Hanging from the immense domed ceiling were the flags of all fifty states. The rail around the rink bore the names and logos of the many corporate sponsors.

"Wow," said George, taking it all in. Out on the ice were about a dozen young female skaters, most accompanied by what appeared to be their coaches. Rinkside, a scattering of observers were carefully watching.

"I'll catch you later," Mike said with a nod before he disappeared behind the bleachers.

Nancy and George nodded back and stepped up to the railing to watch the skaters. "Wow," Nancy repeated. The skaters were gliding confidently over the ice, but every now and then one of them would leap suddenly into the air. She would turn or twist or kick in ways that seemed impossible but obviously weren't—not for skating champions, anyway.

"I'm already impressed," Nancy murmured appreciatively.

"There'll be some fifty skaters competing in all," Kevin explained. "Some will skate alone—

what they call singles. There are separate competitions for women's and men's singles. Then there'll be pairs skating and ice dancing."

"What's the difference between pairs skating and ice dancing?" Nancy wanted to know.

"In pairs skating, a man and woman do an athletic routine together," Kevin told her. "Ice dancing is just that—dancing on ice. A couple has to demonstrate that they can do the tango, polka, rumba, and other dances on the ice."

"The top four skaters or pairs in each category will go on to the world championships in Berlin," George added.

"We forgot to tell Nancy about the compulsories," Kevin reminded George. "A skater is required to cut into the ice various figures that resemble two- and three-lobed eights. It's the most old-fashioned way to judge a figure skater. I hear the federation is eliminating them, but these competitors will still have to do them."

"Visitors! Press people! Coaches! May I have your attention, please?" A voice came over the intercom. "Please gather at the south side of the rink for orientation."

Two well-dressed women were in the stands at the south end. They seemed to be organizing a large stack of white folders.

"That means us," said Kevin. "They're probably going to hand out passes now. I've already asked my producer if you two could have passes, and he agreed to it."

"Fantastic!" George said brightly.

"Thanks a lot, Kevin," Nancy added. "This is really great of you."

"Hey," Kevin said with a grin, "what are friends for?"

The three of them walked along the rubber matting that covered the floor near the railing to where the other onlookers were gathering.

When most of the visitors had assembled, a tall, striking blond woman of about thirty-five raised her hands, signaling everyone to settle down.

"That's Kathy Soren," George whispered in Nancy's ear. "She was a gold medalist twenty years ago."

"Hi, everyone, and welcome," the former champion said with a smile. "My name is Kathy Soren, and I'm with the American Skating Federation. I'd like to take a moment to go over some ASF ground rules with you before the general public arrives.

"Security is very important to everyone at an event as large as this one," Ms. Soren said. "That's why the ASF has allotted just two passes per skater for people he or she most wants or needs on the scene. We've tried to limit press passes, too. Anyone without a pass will be admitted into the arena only when the general public is allowed. So please, respect the privilege you are being given by making sure your pass is in plain view at all times. We don't want people without passes wandering around the complex."

"I've heard they're very security conscious this

year because of the new scoreboard," Kevin whispered.

"What new scoreboard?" Nancy asked. Before Kevin could reply, Ms. Soren continued speaking.

"Next," Ms. Soren said, "our skaters will be under tremendous pressure during the next few days, and it's imperative that you remember that. I'm especially talking to the press here. Some skaters love publicity; others hate it. So if a skater needs privacy, please respect that." Kathy Soren gave the group a stern look, then broke into a warm smile. "Okay, I've said my piece. Now I'm going to turn you over to my assistant, Myra Becker. She'll hand out your passes and answer any questions you may have. Enjoy the competition!"

With a quick wave, the gold-medal winner stepped down from the bleachers. She headed for a slightly elevated platform facing the middle of the rink, on which sat a long table and a single row of chairs. From the way it was positioned over the ice, Nancy assumed that was where the judges would sit.

"What exactly is the judging based on?" a man asked from the back of the group. He had a beard, and Nancy thought she detected a faint German accent.

Kathy Soren's assistant pushed her oversize glasses back onto the bridge of her nose and answered. "Basically, every category, except for the compulsories, is judged for both skill and artistic expression. Compulsories are marked only for skill. Six is the highest score, zero the lowest. When the scores come in, the ASF committee discards the single highest and lowest scores and then averages the rest. The fine points of scoring are all outlined in the information pack I'll be handing out."

"Can we talk to the judges if we have a question?" a woman with brassy blond hair and heavy makeup asked. From the way she poised her pencil to note down the response, Nancy guessed she was a reporter.

"That's a good question," the ASF representative said with a laugh. "And the answer is no! Referees are the *only* people permitted to speak to the judges. Everyone else, including skaters, coaches, and the press, is strictly forbidden to have any direct contact with them."

There were no more questions, so Myra began handing out the program packets and passes. Each thick white envelope was marked separately. "Here are the Worldwide passes," she said, handing about a dozen envelopes to Kevin.

"Thanks," he said. He fished out envelopes with George's and Nancy's names on them and handed them to the girls. "Here you go," he said.

Opening her envelope, Nancy found a clear plastic card holder with her name on a piece of paper inside. On the back of the holder was a large pin.

George was already pinning her pass to her sweater. "Now you look official," Kevin said with a laugh. "Well, I'd better start earning my pay. See you later." With a wave to Nancy and a quick kiss on the cheek for George, he was off.

"Let's watch the skaters from over there," George said, pointing to a spot by the railing.

"Looks like Kevin's going to be really busy for the next few days," Nancy commented, leafing through the glossy program that accompanied her pass. "There's a lot going on."

"He already warned me about that," George said. She frowned slightly as they made their way to the railing. "But at least there'll be plenty to keep us busy too."

The first skater Nancy noticed was spinning rapidly, first on one leg, then the other. A bright red cap had been tugged down over her sleek black hair, and the red and black blurred as she continued to rotate. "Look at that girl in red. Who is she?"

"That's Veronica Taylor. She won the nationals last year," George said, "but she didn't place at the world championships. This year may be her last chance. She's almost twenty-four, and in skating that's practically ancient."

"Look, Dad. There's Veronica!" came a bright voice behind Nancy.

Nancy turned to the speaker, a tall, slim red-haired girl with a long mane of bouncing curls. "George, isn't that Trish O'Connell, the skater we saw last year at the River Heights skating exhibition?" she asked.

"It sure is," George said excitedly. Trish had

captivated everyone in the girls' hometown with her skating ability and her warm, bubbly personality. Behind her walked a well-dressed man Nancy assumed was her father. He was about fifty, with short gray hair and bright blue eyes.

"Hi, Trish," George said brightly.

"Hi," Trish answered with a cautious smile, trying to place George. "Are you family or friends of one of the skaters?"

"No, we're just fans," George answered. "I'm George Fayne, and this is my friend, Nancy Drew. We saw you skate in River Heights."

Just then, Veronica Taylor skated up to where they all were standing. Nancy observed that up close Veronica was even more beautiful than she had appeared on the ice. She had clear skin, large dark eyes, and full red lips. "Trish, hi," Veronica said, smiling at the red-haired girl. "Did you just get here?"

Trish nodded. "Yes, and guess what? Dad arranged for us to share a hotel room. Isn't that great?"

"But I was going to the local YWCA," Veronica replied. "A hotel will cost a for—"

Trish's father put up his hand to stop her. "It's on me," he announced. "I want both of you to be comfortable for the next few days, so it's worth the money. After all, Ronnie, you're practically part of our family."

"Well, thanks," Veronica told him, smiling. "That's really generous of you."

"Veronica, this is George Fayne and Nancy

Drew," Trish said. As she said Nancy's name, Trish hesitated slightly and her green eyes fixed on Nancy. She tilted her head to one side. "Wait a minute! Are you *the* Nancy Drew? The famous detective?"

Nancy could feel herself turning red. "I don't know how famous—"

"Pleased to meet you!" Trish said excitedly, taking Nancy's hand and turning to her father. "There you go, Dad. If you have any problem with your Optoboard you can get Nancy to help you!" She turned back to Nancy proudly. "I'd like you to meet my father, Brett O'Connell. Dad is the president of Fiber-Op Corporation. They invented the Optoboard."

"I'm still not sure what that is," Nancy said.

Trish's father spoke to both Nancy and George. "Basically, it's a marriage between digitalized computer images and rudimentary hologram theory."

"Oh, Daddy," Trish said with a giggle. "Let me tell them in plain English." She turned to the girls. "The Optoboard is a really amazing scoreboard and video monitor rolled into one. And get this—the pictures are three-dimensional! It looks like they're popping out at you."

"I can't wait to see it," George said.

"It hardly uses any power at all, because it all runs on one little circuit board," Trish added.

"Trish is my biggest fan," Mr. O'Connell said. "I do have to go check on a couple of things—so, ladies, if you'll excuse me . . ." Mr. O'Connell made his way around the edge of the ice.

"Excuse me, but I need to leave, too. I have to practice," Veronica broke in. "I've got only five more minutes of ice time. I'll meet you in the locker room, Trish. 'Bye, everyone!"

Wearing a pleasant smile, Veronica wove backward on her skates as Nancy and George watched appreciatively.

Nancy's smile disappeared a moment later when Veronica's foot lurched out suddenly. Nancy gasped as the pretty skater fell back, hitting her head on the ice with a painful crack.

"Oh, no!" George cried, grabbing hold of Nancy's arm. "Nancy, she's hurt!"

Chapter Two

"OH, NO!" Trish echoed George. She slid out on the ice and bent down next to Veronica, who was holding her head.

"Good, here comes help," Nancy observed. In seconds a team of emergency medical personnel surrounded the dark-haired skater. They asked Nancy, Trish, and George to leave the ice.

"Can you see anything, George?" Nancy asked from behind the railing.

"No," George replied tensely. "I hope she's okay. That fall was nasty."

Nancy frowned. "Definitely. In fact, it looked downright odd. I mean, how many great skaters do you know who fall doing something so simple? It seemed like something stopped her cold."

Nancy turned as two girls skated up to the railing and moved around behind it. One was a tall, graceful girl who was about eighteen. Her white blond hair was tied back in a long ponytail. The other was a petite dark-haired girl about sixteen with pert straight bangs framing her face.

"What a terrible fall!" the petite girl cried. "Did you see her go down, Trish?"

"She just sort of flipped back," Trish said.

"It looked nasty," the blond skater said nervously. "I hope it wasn't anything I did to the ice."

"Pardon?" Nancy leaned toward her.

The blond girl looked at Nancy as if seeing her for the first time. "Like, if I cut a deep rut in the ice or something," the girl explained.

"Elaine was practicing on that patch right before Veronica," the other girl added.

"Look!" George broke in. "She's getting up!"

The medics were helping Veronica to her feet. She was obviously in pain, but she seemed to be moving all right. The medics led her across the ice to the holding area on the south end of the rink, and then out toward an exit ramp.

"Thank goodness," Elaine said.

"Look, Elaine," said the petite dark-haired skater. "There is something out there on the ice, right where Veronica fell!" Without waiting for a reply, she sped out onto the ice.

"Yoko, wait!" Elaine called after her, but Yoko

was already at the spot where Veronica had fallen. She bent down, picked something up, and stared at it quizzically. She skated back to the others, holding out her hand with what she'd found.

"A paper clip?" George said, puzzled.

"May I see it?" Nancy asked. Yoko dropped it into her hand.

"That's funny," Elaine said. "Why would there be a paper clip on the ice? A hair clip, I could see. We all wear them. But a paper clip?"

"Maybe one of the judges dropped it," Yoko suggested. "I saw Mr. Fleischman out here before."

"Yes, but the Zamboni machine swept the ice clean after that," Elaine reminded her.

Trish checked in the direction of the exit ramp down which the medics had taken Veronica. "Let's go see if Ronnie's okay," she suggested.

"Right." Elaine shoved off onto the ice, followed by Yoko. Trish jogged along the rubber matting around the outside of the rink.

George stared after the three skaters. "They seem nice, don't they?" she commented. "Not like ruthless competitors, that's for sure. I mean, the way that girl Elaine worried that it might have been her fault—"

"It couldn't have been her fault," Nancy put in. "A rut in the ice wouldn't have stopped a skater cold. This paper clip, though . . ." She turned it over in her hand thoughtfully.

"There's Kevin," George said, pointing up to

the press box that hung out over the bleachers. Kevin was standing behind a large Plexiglas window, motioning to them. "He wants us to go up there," George added excitedly. "Cool! Come on, Nan."

The girls walked along the front row of seats to an archway that led to the arcade behind the stands. Lining the arcade were the concessions, restrooms, and escalators to the balcony and bleacher seating. George led Nancy to a small, unobtrusive elevator. After showing their passes to a guard, they rode up one flight to the press level.

"Kevin told me the VIPs and the lighting and sound people are all up here," George told Nancy as the door opened onto a curved hallway with thick red carpeting.

They passed a door with two security men guarding it. "'Optoboard Control Room,'" Nancy said, reading the sign on the door. "Whoa. Top secret, huh, George? Can't wait to see this Optoboard in action."

As they continued moving along the circular hallway, George became perplexed. "Wait a minute. Where do we go, Nan?" she asked. "I'm lost."

Nancy shrugged. "Let's keep going this way," she said.

Just then a man came barreling out of a doorway on their left, crashing right into Nancy. She stumbled backward and caught herself against the wall. Her eyes met those of the startled reporter she'd noticed at the orientation earlier—the one with the beard and the foreign accent.

"I'm sorry," he tossed out. "I seem to be lost. Do you know where the press lounge is?"

"Sorry," Nancy told him. "We haven't been on this level before."

"Oh, well," he said with a sigh. "I'm sure I'll find it if I keep looking." He went down the hall in the direction from which the girls had come.

Nancy and George shrugged at each other. Nancy then took in the sign on the door the man had barreled out of. "Danger! Keep Out!" was printed on it in bold red letters.

"Maybe he can't read English?" George suggested, following Nancy's gaze.

"I doubt it," Nancy said. "He's supposedly a reporter, and he certainly speaks English well enough. I wonder what's in that room?"

"Maybe Kevin will know. There's the Worldwide control room," George said, quickening her step and pointing just ahead. "I see their sign on the door."

Inside, Kevin was leaning against the wall, talking to Mike, who was holding a small video camera and tripod. When Kevin saw the girls poke their heads in the door, his face lit up with a smile.

"There you are. Great!" Kevin said. "Listen, I'm hoping you can help me with something."

"Sure," George said. "What's up?"

"I'd like to line up some interviews with the

women skaters, but they tend to hang out in the women's locker room. Would you do me a favor and go down there to see if anyone's willing to give me an interview?"

"Sure," George said, grinning at her boyfriend. "Anyway, I'd love to see what champion skaters are like off the ice."

Kevin nodded. "This should be a great time to get them all together. Otherwise, I'll have to run all over tracking them down individually."

"We'll be happy to help," Nancy said.

"Terrific," Kevin replied with a grin. "I'll get my schedule and a pen and we can go right now. Feel free to grab a sandwich in the meantime."

While Kevin fished through a nearby desk for a pen, Nancy and George each picked up a sandwich from a table against one wall. As Nancy munched on her tuna, she took a quick peek past the large black TV cameras and through the bank of windows that looked down on the arena. "What a view," she murmured, taking in the rink below.

At the moment there were no skaters on the ice. Instead, a group of workers was busily rolling out a large scaffolding unit.

"They've shut the rink down for the next few hours so they can finish installing the Optoboard," Mike explained.

"You'll have a perfect view of it," George remarked.

"So will everyone else," Kevin said. "At least that's what the people from Fiber-Op claim.

They say that when those three-dimensional figures appear, they'll be visible from every seat in the arena." He clipped a pen onto his jacket pocket.

"All ready?" George asked Kevin. He nodded and pushed open the door for her and Nancy.

"There's an elevator right out here," he said, leading them to the left.

"Kevin, what's in that room down the hall marked Danger?" Nancy asked as they stepped into the elevator.

"I don't know," Kevin admitted. He turned to Mike, who shrugged.

"We saw a reporter coming out of there and wondered what he was doing," Nancy explained.

"Maybe he was really lost, like he said," George commented. "Give that detective brain a rest, okay?"

Nancy smiled. "Okay. You're probably right."

Soon they were on the lower level, following signs to the women's locker room.

"Try to chat with them a little," Kevin advised George. "Let them know I won't take up much of their time or anything, okay?" He paused at a large oak door marked Women Only. "Here you are," Kevin announced.

"Wish us luck," George said. She turned bright red as Kevin bent to give her a kiss. With a final wave to Kevin, the girls pushed through the door.

The spacious locker room was immaculately clean and appeared to be freshly painted. There were long hardwood benches in front of rows of turquoise lockers. Between groups of lockers were large mirrors with small, laminated shelves at the sides.

The first person Nancy saw was Veronica Taylor, because the skater was lying on a bench against the back wall straight ahead of them. Under her head was a small folded towel and an ice pack. Her eyes were shut, and she appeared to be sleeping.

Trish O'Connell was standing at a mirror almost right beside the door, fluffing her red curls with a wide-tooth comb.

"Knock, knock," Nancy said loudly enough to get Trish's attention. "Mind if George and I come in?"

"Of course not," Trish said with a smile.

"How's Veronica doing?" she asked, stepping farther inside, with George close behind her.

"She's got a mean-looking bump, but the medic said she'll be fine," Trish answered. "She's resting now."

"We've been asked to deliver a message to all the skaters," George said.

Intrigued, Trish called out loud to everyone. "Listen up. For those of you who haven't met them, this is George and Nancy. They want to tell us something."

The other skaters peeked out from various locations around the locker room. Yoko and Elaine were there, and Nancy recognized a few of the others who had been practicing earlier. There were Suzanne Jurgens, who skated in both singles and pairs; Alicia Mendez, winner of the Southwest Division championship; and Heather Lupton, from Vermont.

"Actually, we want to *ask* you something," George explained. "Kevin Davis, a reporter from Worldwide Sports, would like to schedule interviews with you. He's waiting outside now, so if you—"

"Kevin Davis?" Veronica murmured foggily. Her eyes blinked open and she raised her head up, wincing. "He's outside the locker room now?"

"Yes," George replied. "If any of you want to schedule—"

George broke off as Veronica swung her legs to the floor and stood up, wobbling slightly. "He's the cutest thing on TV!" she said, checking herself out in a nearby mirror. "How do I look?"

Before anyone could answer, Veronica tossed her dark silky hair back over her shoulders and made her way a bit unsteadily to the door.

"Ronnie, shouldn't you be lying down?" asked a freckle-faced skater who appeared to be about thirteen years old.

"Oh, it's okay, Terri," Veronica said. "I feel better now. It was just a little bump." With that, she was out the door.

"That was an amazing recovery," George murmured under her breath. Nancy noticed that George wasn't particularly happy.

"Good for Veronica," said Trish, pulling her hair back with a clip. "Maybe arranging an interview will cheer her up. She could use something good to happen to her right about now."

"You mean because of that fall?" Nancy asked.

"Well, that," Trish said, "and also what happened to her coach."

"What happened?" George asked.

Yoko joined in the conversation from the bench where she was sitting. "She just found out he's got pneumonia," she volunteered. "He won't be able to be here at all."

"Which is about the worst thing that can happen to a skater," added a pert girl with short curly brown hair. Nancy recognized her from her picture in the program as Ann Lasser from Florida. "We really depend on our coaches during a competition."

"Veronica doesn't have anybody here to give her any moral support, either," Trish added. "Her folks died in a plane crash a few years ago, and the aunt she lives with couldn't make it to the competition."

Nancy shook her head slowly. "She hasn't had it very easy, has she?"

"No," Trish told her. "But don't feel *too* badly for her. I've known Ronnie since I was six years old and she was ten. She always bounces back. She's very resilient."

"I noticed that," George said with a frown. "The way she bounced right up at the mention of Kevin's name was very resilient."

"Come on, George," Nancy suggested. "Let's go out and see how they're doing. We'll catch you later, okay?" she told the other skaters. "And please, go see Kevin. He's out there now with his appointment book."

Waving goodbye to the skaters, Nancy and George stepped back out into the corridor. Nancy watched as George immediately stiffened her spine. A few feet away Veronica was standing so close to Kevin that she seemed to be pressed against him. She was smiling up at him with an adoring expression.

"George!" Kevin said with a trace of discomfort in his voice. He stepped away from the pretty skater and fixed his eyes on George. "How'd it go? Is anybody else going to sign up for an interview?"

"It went just *fine,*" George said, her jaw clenched.

Veronica turned from Kevin to George. Then she covered her mouth with her hand. "Oh! I didn't realize—"

"I'll see you tomorrow," Kevin told Veronica in a businesslike voice. Then he took George's arm and led her down the corridor. Nancy stayed behind, guessing that he wanted to be alone with George to explain what had just happened.

"I had no idea that he had a girlfriend," Veronica said, acting totally embarrassed. "I guess I *was* flirting, a little. Your friend won't be mad, will she?"

"I doubt it," Nancy answered. "George isn't the jealous type. Anyway, how could you have known?"

"Oh, well," Veronica said with a guilty smile. "He is adorable, though." She slipped her hands deep into the pockets of the oversize red sweater she was wearing over her black leggings.

"What's this?" Veronica said, pulling a sheet of paper out of one of her sweater pockets. She glanced at it and shock registered on her face. "Nancy, look at this," she said in a barely audible whisper, holding the paper out to her.

Nancy stared down at the bold block letters: VERONICA TAYLOR, GET OUT OF THE CONTEST NOW. YOU'RE SKATING ON THIN ICE.

Chapter Three

VERONICA, how long could this paper have been in your pocket?" Nancy asked.

The skater's voice shook as she replied. "I—I really don't know. I took the sweater to the rink this morning in case I got cold and just threw it over the railing near where I was working."

"Do you have any idea who could have written this?" Nancy probed, searching the skater's face.

Veronica bit her lip and hunched up her shoulders. "I have absolutely no idea. I hate to think it could be one of the other skaters. We have too much in common to try to hurt one another. I mean, even though we're competitors, I like to think we all hope for the best for one another."

"I understand," Nancy said, staring at the note in her hands. "But maybe—just maybe—not everyone feels that way."

Veronica took a deep breath and slowly let it out. "I probably shouldn't mention it, but I know Elaine doesn't like me very much," she said. "She can't stand the fact that I beat her at the nationals two years in a row. But I don't think she'd ever . . . " Veronica's voice trailed off and she stared at the ground.

"Well, it doesn't matter who wrote it. I think you'd better be careful," Nancy said, handing the note back to the skater.

"Boy," Veronica murmured, "if someone is trying to shake me up, they certainly are succeeding. Between that fall and this note, I'm getting really spooked!"

"Yoko found a paper clip on the ice," Nancy told her. "That's why you fell."

Veronica's dark eyes widened. "What! There was a paper clip on the ice? But everyone who works for the federation makes sure there's no debris on the ice."

"Well, either they goofed or somebody tossed it there so you'd fall," Nancy said.

Biting her lip, Veronica whispered, "Promise me you won't mention any of this to Kevin or anyone else in the press, okay? Something like this reflects badly on all of us. Besides, maybe if I just ignore it, this stupid stuff will all stop."

"I hope you're right," Nancy replied, trying to keep the skepticism out of her voice.

"I mean, the last thing I need is one more upsetting incident," Veronica went on. "Tomorrow are the compulsories. They're my weakest area, even when my coach is around. I really need to concentrate on my skating, not on some stupid note."

"I can imagine," Nancy said sympathetically.

"I'd really appreciate it if you'd come watch the compulsories," Veronica said, almost pleading with Nancy. "They're the first thing tomorrow. I heard Trish say you're a detective, and I'd feel better knowing you're around."

"If you think it'll help at all, I'll be there," Nancy promised.

"But, Nan," George lamented the next morning as the two girls drove to the arena from River Heights. "If you go to the women's compulsories, you'll miss the free-style pairs skating! Kevin even said we could watch from the Worldwide press box."

"I hate to miss the pairs," Nancy said, "but I promised Veronica I'd be there. After her fall and that note, she's feeling extra vulnerable."

"I wonder who could have written that note," George mused. "Somebody must really have it in for her."

"See what you can find out today, okay?" Nancy urged, as she rolled down her window to take a ticket from the parking-lot attendant.

"Of course," George said with a grin as Nancy

pulled into a vacant space. "I'll look for you after the first part of the pairs program. It says in the press kit there'll be a break late in the morning."

"Great," Nancy said as she and George headed for the staff entrance. "Meet me at the small rink then," she told George. "It's in the east wing."

"If they have a break in the compulsories at the same time we can check out the restaurant in the west wing. Kevin said it's pretty good," George said. With a wave, George hurried into the main rink, while Nancy went around to the east wing.

The smaller rink was just that—smaller than the main one, though it was still quite large. Nancy arrived just as the compulsory event was about to begin. She could feel the tension in the room. Nine judges wearing white ribbons stood on the ice, just inside the railing, talking quietly with each other. On the far side of the rink, waiting in a nervous little cluster, were the male singles skaters.

Too bad for you, George, Nancy thought to herself with a smile. You missed a close look at a bunch of gorgeous guys!

Checking the stands, Nancy was surprised at how few onlookers there were. Just a few dozen people had come. Nancy guessed that most of them were probably connected to the skaters, and the others were reporters. The general public would be far more interested in the music, costumes, and spectacular skating of the pairs competition.

Nancy scanned the rink for Veronica or any of the other female skaters, but they hadn't emerged from the locker room yet.

"The men's compulsories will be our first event," a voice over the loudspeaker told the spectators. "We ask for absolute quiet during the figures, so the skaters can concentrate fully. Skaters will be judged by the shape they trace on the ice and the smoothness of the cut they make. Each of the nine judges will score the competitors on a scale from zero to six. The high and low scores will be dropped, and the total of the remaining seven scores will be multiplied by a factor and credited to the skater. Starting the program will be Boyce Miller."

Breaking away from the group of men, a tall, handsome blond skater slid onto the ice. He gave a quick wave and wink to an older couple in the stands. Nancy guessed they were his parents.

Nancy moved closer to the holding area to see if any of the girls she'd met were there. Ann Lasser and a few others had emerged from the locker room and were now sitting on a long low bench, waiting patiently for the women's competition to begin.

Next the judges were introduced. A tall, heavyset judge named Gilbert Fleischman spoke into a microphone attached to the judges' station that had been set up on the ice, right inside the railing. "Mr. Miller, please begin with a back inside eight."

From her program notes, Nancy knew that a

back inside eight meant that the skater had to cut the figure on the inside edge of his blade while moving backward.

Releasing a deep breath, the handsome young skater bent his knee and began gliding. He started etching a figure eight into the ice with one strong, smooth, careful motion.

Nancy watched intently until harsh whispers to her left distracted her from the action on the ice. Nancy saw Yoko sitting in the stands next to the holding area with a red-haired man who was wagging a finger in her face.

"I haven't worked this hard with you for you to mess up now," he told the skater sternly. "The way you skate is a reflection on me, remember."

"But, Brian, I'm doing my absolute best," Yoko protested.

Her coach glanced in Nancy's direction and saw that she was listening. "I'm leaving," he muttered, turning back to Yoko. "I'm extremely upset with you right now, and I don't want to throw you off."

"Honestly," Yoko pleaded. She looked as if she might cry. "I was here at six this morning. I know you wanted me to start at five, but it's too early! I really needed the extra rest."

Her coach shook his head, frustrated, and muttered, "See you later. Good luck." Then he got up and walked out of the rink.

Yoko immediately got up and walked over to the holding area. Nancy could see that she was deliberately avoiding eye contact with anyone.

She was obviously embarrassed by her coach's behavior.

A quick burst of applause brought Nancy's attention back to the action on the ice.

"Now, a double three, please," Gilbert Fleischman was saying.

After that figure and one more, Boyce was asked to leave the ice while the judges assessed his performance. All nine judges walked out on the ice, inspecting the various figures. Moments later, after their scores had been calculated, Boyce Miller's score was announced. From the applause, Nancy guessed that it was extremely high for compulsories.

Nine more men followed, but none of them matched Miller's score.

"We'll begin the women's program now with the first five contestants," Gilbert Fleischman announced when the men had finished. "Then we'll break and come back to finish the compulsory competition. Will Yoko Hamara come forward first, please?"

Yoko suddenly appeared on the ice. The worried expression was gone from her face, replaced by a wide smile. She skated to the far end of the rink, where a Zamboni machine had just resurfaced the ice.

Fully concentrating, Yoko went from one figure to the next, drawing delighted "aahs" from the small audience as she finished each one. Her total score was excellent.

Veronica Taylor was next. She smiled nervously at Nancy as she slid onto the ice to begin her figures. Compared to the day before, when Nancy had watched her practice her freestyle program, Veronica's skating was stiff and awkward. When she was finished, she skated to the railing and waited for her score. Disappointment was expressed on her face.

After Fleischman announced Veronica's score, the girl slumped back against the railing. Nancy could see the tears in her eyes.

Suzanne Jurgens was next, followed by Ann Lasser. They were just behind Yoko, but well ahead of Veronica. Even the last skater, Terri Barton, scored above Veronica. Reading from her program, Nancy learned that Terri was only fourteen years old, one of the youngest people ever to compete at this level.

"The judges have asked for a short break," came Kathy Soren's soft voice over the microphone when Terri was finished. "We will resume in five minutes."

Nancy walked over to the spot outside the rink where Veronica was standing. "Last place!" Veronica muttered bitterly. "I could just scream!"

Nancy put a comforting hand on the skater's wrist. "Come on, Veronica," she reminded her, "the compulsories are only one part of your overall score. You can still win the gold."

"Thanks," Veronica said smiling weakly.

Soon, Kathy Soren tapped on her microphone. "We'll resume the compulsories now with Trish O'Connell."

Nancy watched as Trish slid across the ice, cutting perfect figures for the judges' inspection. When she was done, Judge Fleischman announced her score and Trish broke into a huge smile. She was in first. She skated over to the railing where her father and her coach, a kind-looking middle-aged woman, both wrapped their arms around her.

"Our next competitor is Elaine Devery," Ms. Soren announced. She turned to the holding area from which the women skaters emerged. Elaine wasn't there.

"Elaine Devery?" the ASF official repeated.

People began twisting their necks for Elaine. Nancy, too.

"Ms. Devery?" The portly head judge tried this time, tapping the microphone that rested on the judges' table.

Suddenly the skater burst from the holding area, wearing a simple green skating outfit. Elaine was standing in her bare feet, with tears streaming down her face. A man wearing a blue jacket and a ribbon marked Referee hurried over to her.

"You'll have to tell the judges that I can't go on!" Elaine wailed to the referee. "Somebody stole my skates!"

Chapter Four

SEEING THE CRESTFALLEN skater standing there, Nancy felt a surge of anger shoot through her. If Elaine's skates really had been stolen, that meant three rotten things had already happened to the skaters in this competition—the sabotage of Veronica, the note to frighten Veronica, and now this. "Somebody's not playing fair," Nancy said under her breath. "And I'm going to find out who."

"Stolen skates? Something juicy to write about," came a raspy voice behind Nancy. "At last!"

Nancy turned and recognized a reporter she'd

first seen when the passes had been handed out. The woman was about forty, with brassy yellow dyed hair and bright red lipstick. A blue-and-red scarf was draped over the collar of her smart red suit.

When she noticed Nancy looking at her, the woman winked. "My paper loves a touch of human interest from these sports events," she whispered before striding over to where Elaine was standing. Nancy followed, annoyed at the reporter's uncaring attitude.

Elaine still stood on the rubber mats in front of the holding area, unable to hold back her tears. Across the rink the referees and judges were conferring.

"Just think," the blond reporter said as she whipped a pad and pencil from her shoulder bag, "all the other reporters stayed away from the compulsories because they're so boring. What luck for me!"

"Not for Elaine, though," Nancy said vigorously. From the front row of the stands, a blond woman in her forties rushed forward to Elaine. Judging from the resemblance between the two, Nancy guessed she was Elaine's mother.

"Honey, where did you last see them?" Mrs. Devery was asking as Nancy and the reporter approached.

"They were in my locker," Elaine said. "I saw them just a little while ago!"

"Who do you think took them, Ms. Devery?" the reporter piped up.

Elaine shrugged her shoulders helplessly. "I have no idea," she replied tearfully.

"Has anything like this ever happened to you before?" the reporter probed.

Shaking her head, Elaine put her face down. "No, it never has."

Nancy couldn't believe the reporter was hounding Elaine this way. Luckily, the referee returned a moment later.

"Okay, Elaine," he explained, "here's what's going to happen. Mr. Fleischman has agreed to move you to the last slot on the program to give you time to get other skates."

"Thank you," Elaine said gratefully. When she turned to her mother, she was still panicky. "Did we bring any other skates, Mom?"

"There should be some in the trunk of the car. I'll go check," her mother replied. She took off for the nearest exit.

"Hi, Nancy," Elaine said quietly.

"Hi," Nancy answered.

Before Nancy could express her concern about what was happening, the reporter moved in closer to the skater. "I've heard that a skater's skates are very special to her. Is it true, Elaine?"

"Yes," Elaine answered.

"Can you tell me why?" the reporter probed. "My name is Fran Higgins, by the way. I write for the *Morning Sun.*"

Elaine was obviously preoccupied, but she managed to answer politely. "It takes months to break in a pair of skates properly. You can't just put on someone else's skates or a new pair and expect to perform well in them."

"Elaine," Nancy broke in gently. "Could the skates possibly be misplaced? Maybe someone moved them by accident. I'd be happy to help you search for them."

"It couldn't hurt," the skater said dubiously, and the two girls turned toward the locker room. Elaine whispered to Nancy, "Thanks for getting me away from that reporter. I didn't know what to say. Part of me just wanted to punch her in the nose!"

When the girls passed in front of Yoko, she jumped up from the stands. "Are you going to look for your skates?" she asked. "I'll help."

"Thanks. I sure hope my mom finds my old skates. Of course, they're practically falling apart," Elaine lamented on the way down the ramp to the lower level. "I haven't had the blades sharpened in ages, either. But I suppose someone can do them here. They'll be better than nothing, and I can perform in them at least."

The three girls turned into the women's locker room, and Elaine marched up to an open locker. "They were right in here," she said, pointing at the empty space. "The door locks automatically. It's a digital combination lock."

"So I see," Nancy said, examining the lock. "Did you program in the combination yourself?"

"No," Elaine answered, "The federation gave it to me." She leaned over to the adjoining locker, punched in four digits, and opened the door. "My costumes are all in this locker, and they're fine."

"Elaine, do you know anyone who might have known the combination?" Nancy asked.

The skater shook her head helplessly. "No, I don't," she answered. "Somebody could have watched me punching in the numbers, I guess."

"That would probably be another skater," Nancy pointed out. "No one else could get close enough to watch without your getting suspicious."

Just then Elaine's mother appeared at the locker room entrance, holding a pair of scuffed skates. "Success! You'll do just fine in these, Elaine," she announced cheerfully. "I'm sure of it." Her worried expression belied her words.

Over the intercom the announcer read another skater's score. It was below average.

"I'd better hurry," Elaine said nervously. "I could be disqualified for lateness. I wish Tess were here."

"Tess?" Nancy questioned.

"Yes, Tess Elkart, my coach. She's getting over the flu."

Turning to her daughter, Mrs. Devery said, "But I know what Tess would say right now. You can cut fine figures in your sleep. You've done them a thousand times before, and on those very skates. You can do them now!"

"Thanks, Mom," Elaine said as she laced up her second skate. Soon she was on her feet, ready to go back upstairs. "Well, it's now or never."

When they arrived at the holding area, Nancy quietly wished Elaine good luck. Then the skater made her way onto the ice. As she took up her starting position, she was concentrated and determined.

Despite her best effort, however, her performance was off. In the first two figures, she lost her balance twice. During her third figure, chipped ice flew up from the back of one skate—a sign that the figure she was cutting would be jagged and rough, not the smooth, fine line that she'd need to score high.

When her score was announced, the worst was confirmed. Elaine was in last place.

From her position near the railing, Nancy saw Elaine's pretty face turn bright red. She felt awful for the skater.

"That ends the compulsory figures competition," the announcer said. "This rink is now available for practice. Thank you."

The spectators began filing out of the rink as the skaters started for the locker room.

"I'd like to know how the judges would do if *their* skates had been stolen!" Nancy heard Elaine's mother complain bitterly.

Since there was nothing she could do to help, Nancy decided to see if George was in the Worldwide press box. Maybe she could catch some pairs skating after all.

After grabbing a hot dog at a stand, Nancy hurried to the main lobby. She showed her pass to the guard, then rode up to the press level. As she emerged from the elevator, a muffled roar from the crowd in the arena filled her ears. By the time she stepped into the Worldwide offices, the cheering was just ending.

Kevin was in a booth, separated from the rest of the room by soundproof glass. He sat in front of a microphone, talking into it. On Nancy's side of the glass, the staff worked their controls. George was there, too, pressed against the window, peering down at the rinks.

When she saw Nancy, George's face lit up. "You can't believe what we just saw, Nan!" she bubbled.

"I wish I had seen the performance that got that last round of applause," Nancy said. "They must have been spectacular."

"They were," Mike told her, leaning over. "And you *can* see them. Watch the Optoboard."

Nancy gazed out into the arena to where the Optoboard was suspended from the ceiling. Highlights of the last performance came on the huge, slightly concave screen, in a dazzling three-dimensional display. "That's amazing," Nancy said, her blue eyes fixed on the screen.

"I've got to see how that thing works," Mike announced excitedly, standing up. "Come on," he said to them. "Let's check out the control room."

"Are we allowed in?" George asked. "I mean, don't they have security guards or something?"

"No problem," Mike told her. "I know the guy who runs the board. We went to school together."

"Don't you have work to do?" George wondered out loud.

"Me?" Mike opened his eyes wide. "Nah. I never work." Then he laughed. "No, really, I'm just hanging around till later. I've got a sound check to do, but I have to wait for the arena to empty out. Dinnertime, I figure." He winked at Nancy. "Otherwise, I would have asked you to join me for a bite."

Nancy grinned. "Thanks," she said. "I'm flattered, but Ned wouldn't appreciate it. George and I *would* like to see the Optoboard, though."

"Ned?" Mike repeated. "Oh, I see. *Ned.* As in, you have a boyfriend." He sighed. "Oh, well, let's go check out that Optoboard, anyway, okay?"

On the way there, Mike said, "According to my friend, the whole Optoboard system operates on a specially designed circuit board smaller than your hand.

"Some little thing, some mere thingamajig," he went on, staring at his palm as if the circuit board were in it, "is what all the fuss is about."

At the control room door, Mike grinned at the security guards. "Could you tell Rob that Mike Campo is here to see him?" he asked.

The guards nodded, and one of them went inside. In a moment he came back out, followed by a thin, pale young man wearing aviator glasses.

"Mike, you dog!" he shouted, clapping Mike around the shoulders. Lowering his voice, he said, "I'm not supposed to let anybody in, but I suppose I can make an exception for you." Then he noticed Nancy and George, too.

"Don't worry," Mike said with a chuckle. "Nancy and George don't want to steal anything. As great as this board is, none of us would have any use for it at home. George and Nancy, this is Rob."

"Hi, Rob," Nancy said. "Do you work for Trish O'Connell's father?"

"Yup," the technician answered. "Step inside." He led them into a smallish booth, then closed the door behind them. On a large table that took up almost the entire space sat a small computer terminal.

"So this is what all the fuss is about?" Mike said, pointing to the terminal.

"*This* is it," Rob answered with a grin. Bending down, he pointed to a box attached to the underside of the countertop. "The circuit board with its newly developed chips fits right in this little slot here."

"Unbelievable," Mike said, shaking his head.

"Hey! Check this out," George said, gazing out the window at the ice below. "That couple is incredible! They're a brother and sister team from Idaho."

Following George's gaze, Nancy watched the couple in red-and-black harlequin outfits, gliding on the ice at breakneck speed to a fast-paced classical violin piece.

As Nancy and the others watched, the music slowed and changed to a romantic tango. The two skaters drifted apart, then drew together effortlessly. After a number of dazzling jumps and spins, the two ended their routine in a brilliant flourish, with the man supporting his partner above his head and spinning rapidly. When he set her down, she landed in a full split, and the music ended.

"Not bad, huh?" Rob said admiringly.

"What are their names?" Nancy asked.

She never got an answer to her question. At that very moment the entire arena was plunged into utter, pitch-black darkness!

Chapter Five

"What happened?" Nancy asked in the darkness.

"It must be some sort of power outage," George said beside her. The blackness was so complete Nancy couldn't even make out her friend's silhouette.

Through the Plexiglas, Nancy heard an anxious buzzing from the arena. "This is very weird," Mike said. "The audience must be freaked."

"Maybe we blew the master circuit breaker," Rob suggested. "But I don't know why." Soft clicking noises told Nancy he was flicking control switches on and off. "I'm not getting anything," he said. "Could the whole town be having a blackout? Maybe there's a storm going on outside or something?"

"It didn't look stormy when we came in," George told him.

"It's strange that someone isn't making an announcement," Nancy observed. "A sports complex this sophisticated has to have an emergency system and plan, don't you think?"

"Of course," Mike said.

"Hey, why don't you guys go see if you can find out what's happening?" Rob suggested. "There's a power room on this level."

Nancy started digging in her purse. "I can't believe I don't have my penlight with me," she groaned. "We'll have to do without."

"Which way do we turn when we get out of here, Rob?" Mike asked.

"Left," the technician answered. "When you get all the way around to the other end, it's almost all the way to the Worldwide press box. It's marked Danger."

Immediately the image of the reporter with the foreign accent who had barreled out of that room flashed into Nancy's mind. "So that room's a power control room," she said to George.

"Uh-oh," George groaned. "I wonder if that guy who bumped into you was fooling around with something in there."

"Come on," Nancy said, groping her way to the door. "Let's go check it out."

"Want to come with us?" Mike asked Rob.

"I have to stay here, no matter what," the Optoboard operator replied. "Mr. O'Connell's orders."

"Well, we'll let you know what's happening as soon as we can," Nancy said, locating the door handle and heading out of the room. "Follow my voice," she told the others. "I'm holding the door open."

The hall, too, was in pitch-blackness, although two faint points of light could be seen bobbing toward them from around the bend. In the next second the source of the light became apparent as the two Optoboard security guards came back to their post. They moved nervously, their flashlights pointing every which way.

"I don't get this," said the older of the two guards, a burly man with dark skin. "One side of this hallway farther on has lights, and the other doesn't."

His partner, a pale, lanky man, nodded. "The lights are out by us, down the whole left side, and in the arena. But if you look at the right side down a ways they're on!"

"We're going to the power room to check it out," Mike told them.

"We're staying right here," the older man said, crossing his arms in front of him. "I don't like this situation at all."

Nancy, George, and Mike continued toward the power room, led by a dim light. By the time they reached it, two bright beams of light came fully into view overhead. The emergency system was obviously working in this area.

"There's the power room," Mike said. A small crowd of maintenance and security people were clustered around it. "I guess they're working on the problem. I'll go talk to one of them. Wait here, okay?" Mike said as he picked his way through the crush of people.

Just then the hall lights came on and the emergency lights faded out. Even in the corridor, Nancy and the others could hear the relieved murmur from the audience in the arena below. A small burst of applause followed.

From the speakers overhead came an announcer's voice. "Thank you for your patience, ladies and gentlemen. Our electrical problem has been cleared up and we will resume our program in five minutes."

The cluster of people around the power control door quickly dispersed.

"Let's stick around a minute," Nancy suggested as Mike walked back over to them.

The last one out of the room was a man with a large toolbox. He reached back to pull the door closed behind him. He hesitated after he closed the door, his hand still on the knob. "That's funny," he said out loud.

"What's funny?" Nancy asked.

The man eyed her ID badge before he shrugged his shoulders and answered. "The door won't lock. Must be something wrong with it."

"Let me have a look," Nancy said, walking up

to the door. She quickly found the reason the door wouldn't lock. "The lock's been fixed to stay open," she announced. "Look at this. It's been taped."

"That explains it!" the man cried. "I thought it was funny that the master switch had been tripped like that and the door was open when we got here. This was obviously a case of sabotage."

"Who'd want to sabotage a skating contest?" Mike wondered aloud.

"Somebody was trying to hurt some of the skaters before this," George told him.

Mike seemed genuinely surprised. "You're kidding!" he said.

"Come on," said Nancy to her friends. "We told Rob we'd let him know what we found out."

On the way back Nancy noticed something sparkling on the carpet. "How did these get here?" she asked, bending down to pick up a half dozen or so shiny blue sequins.

As Nancy stood examining the sequins, one of the Optoboard guards came toward them from a hallway off to the left.

"What's going on?" Nancy asked. "Aren't you supposed to be guarding the control room?"

"During the blackout, we heard a woman screaming for help down that corridor," the thin guard answered. "But when I went to check it out, I didn't find anybody!"

"Oh, no," Nancy said, dread shooting through her. "We've got to get to Rob right away! He may be in danger!"

"In danger?" Mike was confused.

There was no time to answer him. Nancy flew around the final curve to the control room. She stopped short when she saw the burly guard slumped to the floor outside the room. The door was standing wide open.

"Rob?" Nancy called as she hurried into the booth. George and Mike were right behind her. There, her worst fears were confirmed. Rob was slouched limply over the keyboard of his computer.

"Rob!" Mike gasped loudly. "Rob!"

"Hmmm?" came the technician's muffled response.

A surge of relief rushed through Nancy. At least he was alive. Out in the hall, the thin guard tended to his partner, who was just coming to.

"Wha . . . ? What happened?" Rob murmured as Nancy, George, and Mike crowded around him.

"Judging from the lump on the back of your head, I'd say someone knocked you out," Nancy told him.

"Whew." Wincing, Rob felt the back of his head. "All I know is, I was sitting here one minute. Then the door opened and someone came in. I thought it was one of you—and, well, that's all I remember."

The two guards came into the control room, the burly, older one rubbing his head. "I didn't see or hear a thing," he said. "Whoever it was hit me from behind."

The lanky guard angrily slammed his palm against the nearest wall. "I can't believe we fell for that trick!"

"We'd better get you two some ice for your heads," George said to Rob and the guard.

All at once Rob seemed to forget about his injury. "Oh, no!" he cried loudly. "The board!" Picking up his head, he stared helplessly at the Optoboard. It was blinking strange patterns and snippets of incomplete information, as three-dimensional shapes jumped crazily across the screen.

"The circuit board," Rob gasped. He reached under the countertop and unhinged the compartment that should have held the board. Instantly his shoulders sagged and he let out a low moan. "It's gone."

"Oh, man," the thin guard said, shaking his head in disgust.

"Do you know who'd want to steal that board, Rob?" Nancy probed.

Still staring at the board, Rob answered wearily, "You name it. There's a lot of money to be made from the board—and its special chips. All sorts of sleazy business types would love to have it without paying for it. That's why we had this elaborate security system!"

Rob turned to Nancy. "How long were you guys gone?"

"About ten minutes," Mike answered for her.

"And I was conscious for probably the first five or so," Rob said. "So whoever konked me knew exactly where to look for the chip. But how?" He rubbed the back of his head. "How did they know?"

"Does this kill the use of the board completely?" Mike asked.

Rob stared at the flashing board as if hypnotized, then he shook his head slowly. "No," he said. "We have a copy of the circuit's design."

"There go our jobs," the older security man moaned.

Nancy shook her head soberly. "It sounds to me like this whole thing was a setup, from the blackout to the woman screaming for help," she said. "Obviously, it was all a ploy so someone could get in here and steal the Opto chips."

"Ladies and gentleman," came the announcer's voice over the sound system. "Welcome back to the pairs-skating program. Last on the ice will be Suzanne Jurgens and Martin Kroll."

As the jaunty couple in matching gold costumes glided onto the ice to take up their starting positions, Mike turned to the others. "I'd better get back to work right away," he said. "I should check out the sound equipment, just in case there was a power surge."

"We'd better call Mr. O'Connell," the burly guard said, walking to the door with the others.

"You guys better clear out, too," Rob told Nancy and George. "I'm fine, really. At least until I talk to Mr. O'Connell."

"Nancy," George said as they headed for the elevator. "Do you think that reporter had something to do with the blackout? I mean the one we saw come out of the power room yesterday?"

Nancy nodded, deep in thought. "Definitely."

"So, where to?" George asked when the elevator door swung open.

"Let's check out the locker room," Nancy suggested. "I want to go through the costumes to see if any of them have blue sequins." She was trying to remember if any of the pairs skaters she'd seen had been wearing blue. She didn't think so, but she couldn't be sure.

"What about that reporter?" George asked.

"If he's the one who stole the chip, he may be long gone," said Nancy. "But if the girl who screamed was his accomplice, and if the blue sequins mean she's a skater, *she's* still around. Maybe we can get to him by finding her."

"She'd have to be one of the pairs skaters to be in costume at that time," George said reasonably.

"Not necessarily," Nancy answered. "Sequins can stick to anything. The skater could be a singles skater who had the sequins stuck on her regular clothes. In fact, my guess is that it isn't a pairs skater, since they were all busy."

Taking the elevator to the lower level, Nancy and George hurried to the locker room. Inside, all was quiet. Only Trish was there, packing up some clothes in a garment bag.

"Hi," she said brightly. "That was some blackout, huh?"

Nancy took a big breath. "Bad news, Trish,"

she said. "The Optoboard chips have been stolen."

"Oh, no!" Trish gasped. "Poor Dad! That's a disaster! I've got to find him right away!" She quickly zipped up her bag and looked around. "Let's see, I've got my costume for my short program, my makeup, and my skates. After what happened to Elaine I decided to take my things home. Did I pack the stuff from my other locker? I'd better double-check." The skater put her bag down on the bench and went to her second locker and punched in the combination to her lock.

"Oh!" she gasped the moment she opened the door.

"Trish, what's wrong?" Nancy asked.

Swallowing hard, the skater stepped aside to show George and Nancy the contents of the locker. "I don't know how this could have happened," she cried.

Hanging by their laces was a pair of snow white skates with shiny silver blades.

"You forgot your skates," George said, reaching for them.

"But I didn't," Trish said, staring at the skates. "Those aren't mine."

Just then Elaine Devery walked into the locker room and smiled at the girls. "Hi, everyone," she said, walking to her locker. "That was some blackout, huh?"

Trish, George, and Nancy were too stunned to

speak. Nancy's eyes went from the skates, to Elaine, and back to the skates again.

Elaine followed Nancy's gaze. In an instant she became furious. Her eyes blazing, she accused Trish.

"Why, you little witch!" she screamed. "You're the one who stole my skates!"

Chapter Six

I'M GETTING a federation official right now!" Elaine shouted at Trish, grabbing the skates from Trish's locker. "I'll make sure you're thrown out of this contest!"

Before Trish could say anything, Elaine stormed out of the locker room.

"Elaine!" Trish cried, running after the other skater. "I didn't take them. Honestly, I didn't!"

George turned to Nancy. "If Trish had taken the skates she wouldn't have opened up her locker in front of us," she pointed out.

"That's exactly what I was thinking," Nancy agreed.

Walking back from the locker room doorway,

Trish pleaded with Nancy and George. "She won't talk to me. I didn't take them—I swear I didn't. You've got to believe me."

"Who do you think did it?" Nancy asked.

Trish shook her head. "I have no idea."

"Well, until you find out who the real thief is," George warned her, "you may be in hot water."

"I know." The red-haired skater leaned against a locker and let out a long sigh. "I can't believe I'm going to get kicked out of the nationals for something I didn't do!"

"Let's go see what we can do about it," Nancy suggested. "Kathy Soren seems like a reasonable person. Maybe we can convince her to hold off doing anything drastic."

Wiping away a tear, Trish nodded. The three girls hurried up to the main arena. Most of the spectators had left for the break between programs. That night, Nancy knew, the men's singles program would pack the stadium.

"I see Elaine talking with Kathy Soren over there," Nancy said, pointing to the front row of seats.

"Thank goodness there are no reporters around," Trish murmured. "If this gets into the news, I'll just die!"

Elaine's mother was at her side, looking angry. As they approached, Nancy could hear Mrs. Devery say, "Okay, I understand why you can't change my daughter's score on the compulsories, but why can't you punish Trish O'Connell?

Shouldn't you throw her out of this contest before she has the chance to steal someone else's skates?"

Kathy Soren seemed very weary as she pursed her lips thoughtfully. "This is a very serious charge you're making," she told Mrs. Devery.

"I didn't steal her skates," Trish broke in. "I would never do anything like that!"

Ms. Soren shot Trish an impatient look. "Her skates were found in your locker," she said. "Can you explain that?"

Trish's lip began to tremble, and Nancy stepped forward. "I think I can, Ms. Soren," she said. "My friend and I were there when the skates were discovered. It seemed to us that Trish hadn't taken the skates. All she had to do was keep her locker shut until we left, and none of us would have guessed the skates were inside. But she opened her locker in front of us, and then didn't even try to hide the fact that the skates were there. She was as surprised to see them as we were."

"I agree," George said.

Ms. Soren looked from Trish to Elaine and let out a big sigh. "Oh, dear," she said helplessly. "This is just what we didn't need."

"I don't see why you're hesitating," Mrs. Devery said hotly. "Trish O'Connell should be thrown out of the competition!"

Ms. Soren put a hand on her hip and shook her head. "Since we can't prove that you took the skates," she said to Trish, "I'm going to allow you—for the moment—to continue in this competition."

"Oh, thank you," Trish said. "I *swear* I didn't take them. I would never do anything so rotten," she added.

Elaine and her mother ignored Trish. "Okay, Elaine," Mrs. Devery said quietly. "We'll just have to abide by that decision." From the strained expression on her face, Nancy thought she was working hard to keep her cool.

"Elaine, I only hope that the real thief is found," Trish said. "Honestly, I didn't take your skates. I didn't even have a way to get into your locker!"

Without looking at Trish, Elaine turned to her mother. "I want to go back to the hotel," she said. "I'm tired."

Elaine's mother put a comforting arm around her daughter's shoulder and shot Trish a poisonous look. "Let's go, honey," she murmured.

Just then Nancy spotted Brett O'Connell walking into the arena from the lobby. "There's your dad," she told Trish.

"Dad!" Trish cried, waving to him. "He's already so unhappy, and now I have to tell him about Elaine's skates."

"Ready to go, Trish?" Mr. O'Connell asked, his car keys in hand.

"Oh, Dad," Trish said. "I have bad news." She quickly filled him in on what had just happened.

Mr. O'Connell seemed distracted as he listened to his daughter.

"What a mess," he said finally, giving Trish a hug.

"This is one of the worst days of my whole life," Trish said, unable to hold back her tears.

"Mine, too," her father said.

"I know." Trish sniffed. "Nancy told me about the Optoboard chips."

"George and I were on the press level when it was taken, Mr. O'Connell," said Nancy as she and George stepped closer to him.

"Some clever ploy that thief used," Mr. O'Connell muttered bitterly. "Setting up my guards like that. They're good men, too."

"Mr. O'Connell," Nancy said. "I have reason to suspect a person I saw here in the arena."

Trish's father raised his eyebrows and stared right at Nancy "Oh? You do?" he asked. "That's right, you're a detective, aren't you?"

"Yes," Nancy replied. "I'm not certain about this, but I saw a man come out of the power room door yesterday," Nancy said. "He was wearing a press pass, and as far as I could tell, he had no reason to be anywhere near that door. I suspect he tampered with the lock so he could cause the blackout to give him cover to steal the chip."

Mr. O'Connell said, "Can you tell me anything else about him, Nancy?"

Nancy gave him a brief description of the man. "He had a slight foreign accent, but he definitely knew enough English to read the sign on the door."

"Foreign accent? What kind?" Mr. O'Connell asked.

"German, I think. Why?"

Trish's father scowled. "Interesting. Lots of firms have a big interest in the circuit board design and the chips, but there's one particular German firm that wants it badly. I'll call my office now and give them your description of the man. Maybe they can come up with a name to match. Too bad we don't have a photograph."

Nancy nodded. "Unfortunately, he's probably long gone by now, and the chips with him."

"Maybe," Mr. O'Connell said. "But maybe not. He might just stay here—it would be the best cover. If this fellow is a well-known corporate spy it won't be easy for him to get out of the country with the chip. Customs keeps a long list of corporate spies, their whereabouts, and their aliases. He'll have to be very clever."

"He's already proven he's clever," Nancy pointed out. "My idea, though, is to keep track of him through his accomplice. If we can find her and get her to confess then we'll have our thief and the proof to hold him."

Mr. O'Connell raised his eyebrows. "The girl who screamed is an accomplice?" he asked.

George nodded. "She left some sequins behind," George put in. "Show him, Nan."

Nancy fished the sequins out of her pocket and held them out to Mr. O'Connell.

His face fell. "These look familiar," he said softly. "Trish?"

"Yes?" Trish came closer and looked at the sequins.

"Aren't these like the ones on one of your costumes?" her father asked.

"I don't think so," Trish said. "I do have blue sequins on my freestyle costume for my long program, but I haven't even unpacked it yet."

Mr. O'Connell was obviously relieved. "Let's talk again soon," he told Nancy. "Right now, I want to make some calls and get some dinner. If you spot that fellow hanging around, try to get a photograph."

"What an afternoon," George said as she and Nancy watched the O'Connells walk off. "Nancy, you don't think she stole those skates, do you?"

"I doubt it, George," Nancy answered.

"Well, we've still got a couple of hours before the men's singles," George said. "Want to catch some dinner?"

"I am hungry," Nancy admitted. "Want to invite Kevin to join us?"

George sighed. "I wish I could, but he said he'd be too busy," she said. "I understand, but I sort of wish he'd find a little time to spend with me."

She looked up into the stands. "In fact, there he is, in the back row, interviewing Ann Lasser."

"Come on, George," Nancy said gently. "Give him a break. Interviewing skaters is his job."

"Well, he sure is an overachiever," George grumbled. "Or at least he was with Veronica. Anyway, I'm famished."

Nancy was glad to change the subject to something neutral. "Me, too," she said.

"Want to try Harper's?" George suggested. "It's not far from here, and Kevin said the food was pretty good."

"Okay," Nancy agreed, starting for the exit. When they stepped outside, Nancy noticed an expensive-looking silver sedan with dark-tinted windows parked at the curb. As they walked out toward the street, Gilbert Fleischman hurried past them with quick strides. He slipped into the passenger side of the car, and, in the next moment, the car drove away.

Nancy stopped short. In the split second that the door had been open, she saw the woman who was behind the wheel of the car. "Fran Higgins was driving that car," Nancy told George. "She's a reporter for the *Morning Sun.*"

"But the judges aren't allowed to talk to the press," George said, her brown eyes opening wide.

"I know," Nancy replied as they continued on their way to her car. "There's a lot of funny business going on around here, George. First, there's a paper clip on the ice. Then, a skater gets a threatening message and another one has her skates stolen. There's the blackout, and the Opto circuit board and chips are stolen."

"And now the judge goes riding off with someone from the press," George added, "which everyone knows is a no-no."

"So what does it all add up to?" Nancy asked, making her way to her Mustang. "If someone is sabotaging the skaters, does it have anything to do with the stolen Opto chips?"

George shrugged. "Beats me," she said.

Nancy opened her car door, got in, and snapped her seat belt, still puzzling over all that had happened. "I didn't think this would happen, George, but somehow, we're in the middle of a case!"

Nancy turned the ignition, and soon the girls were off, riding toward the town of Montgomery. Harper's was conveniently located on the main street, just at the edge of the downtown area.

"This looks nice," George said after they entered the restaurant. A sign propped up on a small table in the entryway read: "Please wait to be seated." Next to the sign were two velvet love seats and a row of large palm plants.

"I wonder where the hostess is?" Nancy said, gazing at the crowded tables.

"Please," a female voice pleaded from behind the plants, catching Nancy's attention. "Please, let's not fight."

The voice sounded familiar. Nancy peered through the leaves of the plants to see Yoko Hamara sitting with her coach and a young man.

"My sister knows her routine upside down and backward, Adderly," the young man was insisting. "She's giving a hundred percent for this competition!"

"A champion has to give more than a hundred percent, Ito," the coach said firmly.

"The way you want to work her, she'll burn out!" Ito Hamara shot back.

"I've gotten her this far." Brian sniffed once.

"Oh?" Ito countered. "Well, I disagree with that. In fact, Yoko might be better off with a coach who'll give her a little respect. Maybe she should think about changing coaches!"

At that Brian Adderly stood up and threw down his napkin. "Oh? Are you threatening to fire me? Just when I've brought your sister to the top levels of competition?" he fumed. "Then all I can say is, do it! Go ahead and ruin her career!"

He turned to Yoko and bent down so that his face was just inches from hers. "Getting rid of me now would be extremely self-destructive, Yoko. Self-destructive and dangerous. If you do it, you'll be sorry. I can promise you that."

Chapter Seven

"NICE GUY," George whispered sarcastically as she and Nancy listened to Brian Adderly's hard-edged speech.

Nancy put a finger to her lips. She wanted to hear the rest of what was being said.

"Oh?" Ito huffed. "So changing coaches would be dangerous? Is that supposed to be a threat?"

"I've had enough of this conversation!" Brian raged. "And I've had enough of your interference, too! Good night!" The coach stalked away from the table just as the hostess walked up to Nancy and George.

"Sorry I kept you waiting," the hostess said with a smile. "Two for dinner?"

"Yes," George answered, her attention on the angry coach who was now walking by them on his way out of the restaurant.

The hostess smiled pleasantly. "I have a booth in the No Smoking section," she said, leading Nancy and George into the dining area. To get to their table, the girls had to pass Yoko and her brother, who sat silently finishing their beverages.

Nancy's heart went out to the petite skater. It had to be hard to have a coach and brother fighting over her.

"Hi, Yoko," Nancy said, pausing momentarily as the hostess continued to lead George to a booth. "Will you be at the men's competition tonight?"

The almond-eyed skater smiled weakly and shook her head. "I'm planning to take a hot bath and get to bed early," she said. "My coach wants me at practice by five in the morning. I lead off the short program."

"Well, if I don't see you before then," Nancy said, "good luck."

"Thanks," said Yoko.

"Oh, by the way," Nancy added, "are you missing any blue sequins from your costume?"

Yoko gave Nancy a puzzled look. "I don't think so," she replied. "My costume is green."

"Okay, then. 'Bye," Nancy said and went to join George at their booth.

George peeked over the top of a large red-and-black menu when Nancy slipped into the booth.

"That Brian seems like a slave driver," George noted. "But do you really think he was threatening Yoko?"

"Maybe not," Nancy replied as she picked up her menu and opened it. "But I suppose you never know with a guy like that. He seems awfully intense and emotional."

"Yum," George interrupted and licked her lips. "They have pasta primavera."

Nancy quickly shut her menu. "Great. I'll have it, too."

"There they are!" came Kevin's voice from the middle of the restaurant. Nancy and George looked up and saw him with the hostess. "Thanks," he told her, then hurried over to Nancy and George's booth. "Hi," he greeted them. "Can I join you?"

"I thought you were busy interviewing skaters," George said, moving so Kevin could slip in beside her.

"I purposely hurried the last interview so I could catch up with you," Kevin said, taking George's hand. "I had a feeling you might be here."

Nancy watched George's expression as she met Kevin's gaze. George definitely seemed thrilled that Kevin had managed to find some time to spend with her.

Kevin scanned the menu and then quickly raised his hand to signal for a waiter. When they'd placed their orders and the waiter had left,

Kevin turned to Nancy. "So, Nancy, you're the detective—who stole the Opto chip?"

"That's the *big* question," Nancy told him, "but it's not the only one."

"Right," George added with a nod. "For instance, who stole Elaine Devery's skates?"

Nancy pressed her lips together thoughtfully and said, "Tonight I want to chat with any of the women skaters who are at the arena, to find out if any of them have blue sequins on their costumes. Maybe you can help me, George."

"No problem," George answered.

"Do you have a camera with you?" Nancy asked. "It would be great to be able to take a picture if we need one."

"Gosh," George said, biting her lip and frowning. "I didn't bring my camera."

"Kevin Davis to the rescue," Kevin said, grinning at them both. "I have an instant camera. It's up in the booth."

"Something tells me we're going to miss all the skating tonight," George said with a sigh.

"Don't worry, George," Nancy said, smiling. "Kevin will be able to get you a videotape of the whole thing, won't you Kevin?"

Kevin's hazel eyes twinkled playfully. "For George, anything," he said.

When they'd finished eating, George rode back to the arena with Kevin, and Nancy used the time alone to think through the Opto chip theft. If Mr. O'Connell was right, and customs was on the lookout for corporate spies, then how did the thief plan to get the chip out of the country?

When she arrived at the arena, Nancy hurried up to the press level, where Kevin and George were waiting for her. "Here's the camera," said Kevin, handing it to Nancy.

Taking the camera, Nancy stepped over to the Plexiglas windows overlooking the arena. "Wow, it's getting crowded," she commented.

"There'll be at least seven thousand people here tonight," Kevin said. "Everyone wants to see Boyce Miller."

"Well, I guess we should get going," George said wistfully, not wanting to leave Kevin. The couple exchanged a quick kiss, then Nancy and George hurried down to the arena.

"If you see any of the female skaters," Nancy said, handing George a few of the sequins from her pocket, "try to get the information without giving anything away."

"Where will you be, Nan?" George asked with a grin. "Watching Boyce Miller?"

"Very funny," Nancy said. "I'll be doing the same thing, unless—" She broke off as something caught her eye. It was the reporter with the German accent and the beard! "George," she said, "I think we just got lucky. Look over there, in the third row behind the judges' station."

George followed Nancy's finger. "It's him!" she gasped.

"I'm going over there," Nancy said, stuffing Kevin's camera into her purse. "Wish me luck."

Nancy hurried around the crowded arena to a seat near where the bearded reporter was seated.

"Excuse me," she said, bumping into him as she slid past him. Then she stopped and looked him squarely in the face. "We met before, remember?" she said. "I'm Nancy Drew, of Worldwide Sports." The man didn't respond, so Nancy went on. "And you are?"

"I'm with the *Berliner Zeitung,*" he told her. "Ernst Schmidt."

"Nice to meet you, Ernst," Nancy said brightly.

The man nodded, giving her a little smile. "If you'll excuse me," he said. Bowing slightly, he stood up and started walking away.

Nancy pulled the instant camera out of her bag and aimed it straight at the back of the man's head. "Oh, Ernst!" she called loudly.

He turned and she snapped his picture. "Thanks. That'll be a nice souvenir!"

The man's face registered shock and fury. "'Bye, now!" Nancy called. She scrambled quickly to the other end of the aisle and joined a knot of people coming up a set of steps.

Success! she thought, her heart beating wildly. Weaving through an incoming throng of spectators, she fled out one of the arena exits. The look on Ernst's face told her one thing for sure—he wasn't happy about having his picture taken. Why would that bother him—unless he was up to something suspicious?

As Nancy moved rapidly toward the front

entrance, she fanned the photo to help it dry. For a split second she stopped to check the image. It was a good, clear shot. Now to get his photo to Mr. O'Connell.

I'm not giving Ernst the chance to get this photo from me, Nancy thought. She headed straight for the parking lot, constantly checking over her shoulder for any sign of the man. She got in her car and drove to the Ridgefield Hotel. She remembered that Trish had told Veronica that was where they'd be staying.

When Nancy arrived, the desk clerk informed her that the O'Connells were out. Disappointed, Nancy put the photo in a hotel envelope and left it for Mr. O'Connell. Then she headed back to the complex. Even if Ernst found her now, he wouldn't get his photo.

Back at the arena, Nancy decided to return the camera to Kevin before going down to the arena. George was sitting in a seat near the skaters' holding area.

"Did you find him, Nan?" George asked when Nancy joined her.

"I sure did," Nancy replied. She quickly filled George in. "How did you do?"

George shrugged. "I talked to Veronica, and she doesn't have any blue sequins—she described her costumes to me in detail. So much detail, in fact, that I've only just got through talking with her. I missed half the program and didn't get to talk to anyone else."

"Don't worry, George," Nancy said. "We'll talk to the others in the morning. Meanwhile, we're still in time to see Boyce Miller—here he comes onto the ice now!"

The next morning Nancy and George showed up at the practice rink just before nine. The place was busy with competitors and their coaches getting ready for the women's short program.

The night before Boyce Miller had sewed up the men's singles competition with ease. He had given the most spectacular performance either Nancy or George had ever seen. In fact, he had so electrified the spectators and other skaters that the air seemed to be charged.

"There's Yoko," said Nancy, pointing out the skater to George. "She doesn't seem the least bit nervous." Against a back wall, Yoko sat on a mat, her eyes closed in what appeared to be deep concentration.

"Well, I know I'd be nervous!" George said.

Elaine Devery was out on the ice, wearing a plain blue leotard and a pair of black bicycle shorts.

"Terrific extension, Elaine," her coach, Tess, said, encouraging the skater as Elaine swung her leg out at a ninety-degree angle and glided in a perfect circle. "It's exactly what we've been going for."

Brian Adderly was pacing on the rubber matting near the rink. Every thirty seconds or so he checked his watch. "Time's up, Tess!" he finally announced. "Yoko is scheduled to work this patch at nine-fifteen."

"Yoko worked the ice for three hours already this morning!" Tess protested.

"The federation gives each competitor ten minutes on the ice the morning before each event," Brian reminded her. "If my skater came early to work out, that doesn't count against the federation allotment."

Annoyed, Tess consulted her wristwatch. "It's only nine-thirteen now," she said.

"Not by the arena clock," Brian grumbled. "You'd better clear the ice."

"One more double back camel, Elaine," Tess instructed, ignoring the impatient coach.

Skating backward along the railing, Elaine leaned into the ice again, so that her arm and torso made a perfect line, twirling swiftly and gracefully. The move was magical.

"I guess the right skates really do make a difference," George murmured.

"Fingertips," Tess called out. In the most delicate of movements, the skater stretched the tips of her fingers into alignment with the rest of her lithe figure. It was the perfect touch for the move. "Nice," Tess said, smiling.

"Excuse me," Brian insisted, in a clipped tone. "My skater is up—*now.*" Snapping his fingers, Brian called for Yoko.

The small girl stretched out her compact, muscular figure. "Please give my time to another skater," she said calmly to Brian. "I feel that any more practice now will destroy the work I did earlier."

Brian stared down at Yoko, aghast. "What do feelings have to do with anything?" he demanded. "This is the American Skating Federation's national competition, or have you forgotten? This is your chance to qualify for the world championships!"

"I know," Yoko said, remaining calm. "And I don't want to burn out before I begin, Brian. I'm going to my dressing room now so I'll have plenty of time to get ready without hurrying."

Brian's face was bright red. He looked from Yoko to her brother, Ito, who sat listening in the front row. Ito's face, too, showed complete surprise at his sister's sudden resolve.

"I'm out of here," Brian finally said, in a bitter tone of voice. "Get yourself another coach!" With that, he stomped to the nearest exit ramp.

"What's going on?" Veronica asked Nancy as she emerged from the holding area, where she'd been lacing up her skates.

"Yoko and her coach just had a fight. She said she didn't want to burn out and gave up her practice time," George told her.

"Great! Maybe I can get it," Veronica said eagerly.

"I don't think so," Nancy said. Suzanne Jurgens had conferred with the referee and was already gliding onto the ice.

"That's not fair!" Veronica complained.

Watching Suzanne, Nancy couldn't imagine that she'd score very high in the nationals. Even though she was an excellent skater and had performed well in the compulsories, she lacked the grace and power of the other competitors.

"Attention please," came a voice over the intercom about an hour later. "The ladies' free-style short program is about to begin. Leading off will be Yoko Hamara."

Nancy felt a thrill go through her as Yoko skated out of the holding area. Smiling confidently, the small skater shot out onto the ice, her powerful legs sending her forward in long graceful arcs as she waved to the crowd. Then she came to a sudden stop, crouching down. The low, long wail of a saxophone played over the sound system.

"What a great beginning," George murmured as Yoko gradually lengthened her body, flying into gear as the music changed to dynamic jazz. Yoko thrust herself into her free skate, totally taking charge of her routine—and of the audience.

"Fantastic," Nancy murmured. The petite skater was a dynamo, gyrating, spinning, leaping! Her skating was punctuated by gymnastic moves that took Nancy's breath away!

"How does she do that?" George wondered, awestruck.

Nimbly, gracefully, Yoko propelled her body high up into the air, twisting and untwisting until she was a swirling blur. The crowd burst into thunderous applause.

Yoko wasn't finished yet. "She still has that triple toe lutz," George reminded Nancy.

"No one will be able to touch this performance," Nancy said. As she spoke, she fixed her eyes on Yoko.

"Here it comes, Nan," George said excitedly.

In the next second Yoko flew into the air, twisting over and over herself. The crowd held its breath, ready to let out a collective cheer.

A second later the crowd only let out a collective gasp as Yoko's foot slipped from under her when she landed. Nancy watched as the skater hit the ice on her back. In painful slow motion, Yoko slid across the ice, her delicate body fishtailing back and forth. Finally, with an ear-splitting crack, her head smacked right into the base of the railing!

Chapter Eight

"OH, NO!" Nancy cried, her voice joining the shouts of alarm throughout the arena.

Yoko's music had come to a triumphant climax, but the skater herself lay frighteningly still on the ice.

"I think she's unconscious!" cried George, horrified.

"Her blade came off, George," Nancy said. "I saw it."

George's eyes narrowed as she absorbed Nancy's words. "But how could anything like that happen?" she murmured.

"That's what we've got to find out," Nancy

replied. "I have a feeling this is another act of sabotage. We've got to get to the bottom of this."

Medics and federation officials had already hurried onto the ice and were kneeling at Yoko's side. From where Nancy and George were sitting, on the far side of the stadium from the judges' station, Nancy couldn't even tell if the fallen skater was breathing.

"Come on, George," Nancy said. Getting to her feet, she made her way past the shaken onlookers in the stands. "Let's get down there."

The two girls wove their way to rinkside, and made it to a place near the holding area. The other skaters had all gathered there, watching the horrible scene unfold before them. The team of medics were lifting Yoko's limp form onto a stretcher and carrying her toward an exit.

Nancy craned her neck and was able to see outside as the large double doors were opened. Outside an ambulance was waiting. She guessed that the federation kept it on call for emergencies such as this one.

"Ladies and gentlemen," came Kathy Soren's voice over the microphone. "Ms. Hamara will receive prompt medical attention. We beg your patience for just a moment until we can resume our program. Thank you."

Shaking his head sadly, Gilbert Fleischman conferred with the other judges.

"She was heading for an all-around perfect score, too, I'll bet," George said sadly.

"Let's go closer to the other skaters," Nancy suggested. "I want to hear what they're saying."

Any differences among the competitors seemed to be momentarily forgotten as they huddled together talking.

"It could happen to any of us, at any time," Suzanne Jurgens said weakly as Nancy and George approached the group.

"I remember the time I broke my leg," Elaine murmured. "It hurt like crazy. Poor Yoko."

"What do you think really happened?" Ann Lasser wondered out loud. "I mean, she was skating so perfectly. You don't just mess up like that."

"Her blade came loose," Nancy put in. "It was detached from the toe end of her boot."

The skaters all turned to Nancy. "I didn't see that," Suzanne said.

"You're right," Elaine told Nancy. "Now that you mention it, I saw her blade swinging loose when they picked her up and put her on the stretcher."

"Have you ever heard of anything like that happening?" Nancy asked the group.

"Sure," Trish replied. "It used to happen to me all the time when I was little. I'd always forget to tighten the screws on the blade."

"Some skaters have two or even three sets of blades for each pair of boots," Suzanne added. "Some blades are better for speed, some are better for figures."

Ann shook her head sadly. "Yoko's such a careful person," she mused. "It isn't like her not to double-check her blade screws before a competition."

No, Nancy thought grimly. It didn't seem like Yoko at all. Although after the fight Yoko had had with her coach, she certainly might have been distracted and upset.

"Are you guys sure her blade came loose?" Trish asked Nancy and Elaine. "Maybe she tripped. One little object on the surface of the ice can make for a pretty bad accident, you know. Look what happened to Ronnie the other day."

The conversation was interrupted by the sound of a powerful machine starting up to their left. Nancy saw the Zamboni about to resurface the ice for the next skater.

"Oh, no!" she cried. "If there is anything out there, the Zamboni will sweep it away. We've got to stop the driver!"

Suddenly she leapt up and waved to get the driver's attention. "Stop!" she cried, leaning over the railing. "Could you just wait for a minute?" Nancy begged the man behind the wheel.

"I got a job to do, miss," the operator told her impatiently.

"Talk to him, George, while I go find the referee," Nancy said. She flew over to where the referee was standing, close to the judges' table.

"Excuse me," she said. "My name is Nancy Drew, and I'm a detective. I have reason to believe that Yoko's accident was purposely caused. May I have permission to check the ice for evidence?"

The referee stared unblinking at Nancy. "You want to do what?" she asked.

"I want to search the ice to see if there is any object on it that might have caused the fall," Nancy repeated.

"How much time will it take?" the referee asked.

"Just a minute or two, I promise," Nancy answered.

The referee frowned at her for a moment, as if sizing her up. "Okay," she finally said, "but if you're not finished in two minutes, I'm going to have to resurface." With that, she signaled to the Zamboni man to hold off on the resurfacing.

"Thanks," Nancy said.

Yoko had been spinning tremendously fast just before she landed and fell, and Nancy realized that the screws could have traveled very far. As thousands of confused spectators watched, she crouched down, concentrating hard on finding the screws that should have been holding Yoko's blade to her boot. Her time was just about to run out when she spied the gleam of something metal near the fiberglass guardrail. She gingerly walked over, taking care not to slip, and picked up two small screws. Then she left the ice and the Zamboni started resurfacing.

Nancy stepped onto the rubber matting and,

avoiding the referee, hurried to where George was waiting, about twenty yards from the skaters.

"The women's short-program skating competition will resume," came Kathy Soren's voice, "as soon as the ice is resurfaced."

"But the contest won't resume for Yoko," Nancy murmured sadly, joining her friend. She opened her hand and showed George the two tiny screws she had discovered on the ice. "This was what I was afraid of, George," she said, grimly. "These screws didn't come loose at all."

George's brown eyes widened. "You mean—"

"Look here. See how one side has grooves and the other is smooth? These screws have been filed down."

George met Nancy's eyes. "Which means—"

"That someone definitely tampered with Yoko's skates," Nancy said. "What happened to her this morning wasn't an accident—it was pure sabotage. Maybe even attempted murder!"

Chapter Nine

"MURDER!" George gasped, staring at the filed-down screws Nancy held in her palm. "That seems unbelievable, but it's true, Yoko could have been killed out there."

"I have to go show this to someone from the federation and the referee," Nancy said grimly. "The police, too, of course. Risking a skater's life is a lot worse than stealing a pair of skates."

"Or even a circuit board," George added, her brown eyes flashing. "Nan, do you think the Opto chips theft is connected to these incidents?"

"I've had the same thought, George," Nancy said, "but I can't put it all together. What do d other people watched Kevin and Veronica they talked casually.

"What do I like to do when I'm not on the ice? , let's see—I guess my favorite thing is being terviewed," Veronica said, laughing.

"That little twerp is flirting again," George umbled.

Nancy had to agree with her friend's assessent. Veronica's behavior was far from subtle.

"Of course, I like going out to dinner and ancing, too. In fact, if you'd like to arrange ome time on the dance floor—" Veronica tilted er head coyly and fixed Kevin with her intense lark eyes.

Kevin cleared his throat, gave a little laugh, hen went on to the next question.

"Give me a break." George rolled her eyes, and he Optoboard changed to a clip of downtown Montgomery, with pictures of the sports comlex under construction.

"Let's go get a cold drink, Nancy," George ggested.

"Good idea," Nancy agreed.

They got up from their seats and walked rough the archway that led to the concessions. ter the girls paid for two sodas, they sauntered er to the wall across from the concession stand drink them.

George," Nancy said quietly. "I can't figure who's responsible for what's going on around ."

stealing a corporate secret and sabotaging a skating contest have in common?"

"There's Kathy Soren," George said, touching Nancy lightly on the arm and nodding in the direction of the former skating champion. Ms. Soren was joining the judges in an informal conference near their platform.

"Let's go show her what we found," Nancy suggested.

"She's going to be shocked," George said as they hurried in the direction of the federation official.

"Ms. Soren," Nancy began, walking up to her. "Can we see you for a moment, please—in private? It's extremely urgent."

The former champion seemed perplexed by the request, but she excused herself. Then she stepped over to Nancy and George.

"I found these on the ice," Nancy explained, opening her hand to show the official the filed-down screws. "They must be the screws from Yoko's blade because the ice was resurfaced just before she went out. But look here—they've been filed down so they'd come loose with enough pressure."

Anger crept over Ms. Soren's face as she peered down at the small metal objects. "I see what you mean," Ms. Soren said. "May I have these, please? I want to show them to Mr. Fleischman and the referee right away." She held out her hand for Nancy to drop the screws in her palm. Then she strode over to where the head judge stood, talking with a referee. Nancy and George followed.

"Excuse me, Mr. Fleischman. These young ladies just found something that you should see," she said. "It's very important."

"Oh?" Fleischman asked nervously, pointedly avoiding Nancy's and George's eyes. "Well, as long as you relay the information for them. I see from their passes that the young ladies are with Worldwide Sports, and I'm under very strict constraints about talking with anyone from the press corps. I don't wish there to be even a hint of impropriety regarding my actions."

The skating official nodded and turned to the girls. "I'll speak with Mr. Fleischman and the referee privately. Please wait a moment."

"Of course," Nancy said politely, stepping a few feet away. When she and George were safely out of earshot, she whispered, "Mr. Fleischman certainly is making a big show of sticking to the rules."

"Yes," George said with an ironic grin, "especially for a guy who was in a car with a reporter just yesterday."

"George," Nancy said more intensely, "if he's not doing the best imitation of guilt I ever saw, he's hiding something—something big. He wouldn't even look at us!"

The judge, the referee, and the ASF official conferred a moment longer before Kathy Soren walked back over to Nancy and George. "Mr. Fleischman told me to tell you that they'll look

into this matter," she said, her mar formal than it had been before.

"Will you be contacting the police asked.

"Yes, we will," she answered hesitan all at once she let out a big breath, as if her guard. "To be honest, girls, Mr. Fle feels we should keep the matter under wr while, to avoid any unpleasant publicit confided to them. "My opinion is that th should be contacted without delay. Since an ASF event, I'm taking the responsibil contacting them."

"Good," Nancy said. "You'd better hang the screws then."

"I will," Ms. Soren said with a tense "Now please excuse me."

As Nancy and George walked back to seats, George shook her head in frust "Things are pretty heavy around here," s grimly.

"That's an understatement," Nancy sitting down to wait for the contest to During the delay in the action, the repaired Optoboard was entertaining th Right now it was flashing cuts of variou interviews with the women singles ska

The image of Suzanne Jurgens d from the screen, followed by a picture ca Taylor seated on a sofa, talking to

"Kevin!" Nancy said, touchin shoulder. But George's attention riveted on the Optoboard. She and

"If you can't, I definitely can't," George replied, shaking her head helplessly.

"Obviously, someone is trying to sabotage the female skaters," Nancy continued. *"And* somebody actually pulled off a major theft, one that can cost the Fiber-Op Corporation millions."

George nodded. "I bet the technology behind the Opto chips will be used in everything in a few years."

Nancy nodded. "Let's just think of who might be trying to hurt the skaters for a minute," she said. "Who have the victims been so far? Veronica—she had the paper-clip accident and the note."

"Elaine had her skates taken," George said, helping construct the list.

"Yoko was set up for a fall with those filed-down screws," Nancy concluded. "That leaves the other seven skaters. Maybe someone is trying to knock out the competition to make sure she qualifies for the World Championships."

"Nancy," George said thoughtfully, "any of the seven could have done it, but some of them aren't in the same class as Yoko or Elaine. They couldn't possibly hope to finish in the top four."

"True," Nancy replied. "The only ones who could really be helped by sabotage are Suzanne Jurgens, Ann Lasser, Terri Barton—"

"And, of course, Trish O'Connell," George finished. "She's the most likely suspect, much as I hate to say it."

"Trish," Nancy repeated, with a sigh. "The skates *were* found in her locker."

"But, Nancy," George said. "Trish is so nice. I can't believe she took those skates!"

"Me, neither," Nancy replied. "Especially after she opened that locker right in front of us. It just doesn't add up.

"Brian Adderly is a possibility. He might have tried to sabotage Veronica and Elaine to help Yoko, then turned on Yoko when she argued with him. But that's pretty farfetched."

"Well, what about Gilbert Fleischman?" George suggested. "He's obviously up to no good, the way he was such a goody-goody about the rules one minute and breaking them the next."

Nancy nodded. "Also, do you remember, Yoko said Mr. Fleischman had been out on the ice before that paper clip was found? Yes, something's definitely going on with him," she said. "But what? What would he possibly have to gain by sabotaging the contest? If he wanted to have a specific skater win, he's in the perfect position to do it by tampering with the scores. He wouldn't have to file down screws or plant objects on the ice."

"Ladies and gentleman, thank you for your patience," came an announcer's voice from the speakers above them. "The short program is now about to resume. Skating first will be Elaine Devery."

"Let's get back inside," Nancy said, finishing up her drink and tossing the cup in the garbage.

"I can't wait to see Elaine's program," George said, doing the same.

The two girls hurried back through the archway and into the stadium. When they got to their seats, Elaine Devery was already standing at the edge of the ice, about to perform. She looked lovely in a powder blue costume with cap sleeves decorated with tufts of tulle. Her dark blue leggings had small gold stars all over them.

George suddenly grabbed Nancy's arm. "Look! She has blue sequins on her sleeves."

"I can't tell from here," Nancy replied, squinting, "but I don't think they're a match for the ones we found. That blue looks different."

"Shhh!" came some voices behind them. Nancy and George were quiet and watched the performance.

Elaine extended one arm gracefully into the air, and chords from Tchaikovsky's *Swan Lake* filled the arena. Elaine swept into her routine, taking the audience with her on a journey of effortless grace and skill. The lyrical music perfectly matched her graceful movements as she twisted and leapt in a beautiful, balletic performance.

Just as the program was building to a climax, a scratching sound was heard over the speakers. Gone were the gentle classical strains. Instead a thundering, ear-blasting rap song shook the building. The bewildered skater came to a halt in the middle of the ice, utter distress and confusion on her lovely face.

"Yo, baby—can I—can I—can I be rude?" came a gruff voice punctuated by the hard beat of a drum. "You're the kind of a girl for a natural dude! Yeow, yeow, yeow, I say, yeow!"

Chapter Ten

"THAT CAN'T BE the music she picked!" Nancy said above the blaring rap song. "Someone changed her tape."

Out on the ice, Elaine waved to the referee and held her arms out in a helpless gesture.

The tape came to a sudden stop as the audience began buzzing.

"Come on, George," Nancy said, getting up and stepping into the aisle. "Let's check out the sound system. The control room is up on the press level."

"Mike Campo can probably show us where it is," George said as she rose and moved into the aisle after Nancy. The girls quickly made their exit under the archway, found the elevator, showed their passes to the guard, and rode up to the press level.

When they entered the Worldwide booth, some of the crew were by the window, staring out. Nancy saw Kevin in his Plexiglas cubicle, and from the red light over his door she could tell he was broadcasting live. Joining the others, she and George peered down at the ice. There, Elaine was finishing her routine without music.

"What's going on?" George asked.

"Fleischman is using his discretion as head judge to make her finish the routine without music," one of the production assistants told her.

"Nice guy," George muttered.

Skating valiantly, Elaine completed her routine, but without the music the performance was empty and uninspired. By the time she glided to a stop, ending on a bended knee with her arms outstretched, she appeared very tense. Although Nancy was too far to be sure, she thought she could detect the skater's chin trembling as she fought back her tears.

With a weak wave to the crowd, Elaine glided off the ice to the holding area, where she covered her face in shame.

Soon the judges held up their scorecards, and a low murmur went through the crowd. "The judges certainly didn't show her any mercy," George said sadly, noting Elaine's poor scores for artistry.

"Has anybody seen Mike Campo?" Nancy asked the Worldwide people.

"He's in the sound room—three doors down," the production assistant said. "He went there the minute we heard the messed-up tape."

Nancy and George headed immediately for the sound room. "Oh, man!" they heard a woman groan as they stepped in through the open door. A woman of about twenty-five was sitting and talking with Mike Campo.

"Mind if we come in?" Nancy asked.

"Of course not," Mike said. He turned to the curly-haired woman and said, "Liz, this is Nancy and George. They're Kevin's friends."

"Hi," Liz murmured listlessly. She propped her elbow on the control panel and rested her chin in her palm.

"Liz is the sound engineer," Mike explained.

"For today, anyway," Liz said. "Tomorrow I'll probably be fired. Hold on, guys. Ann Lasser is up. I've got to put her tape on."

Out on the ice, Ann Lasser, wearing a red-and-yellow outfit, skated out of the holding area. Liz put her hand on the control of a large reel-to-reel tape recorder in front of her and waited for the skater to get into position. "Here we go," Liz murmured, setting the tape in motion. "Let's hope this is the right music."

Fortunately, it was. Bright circus music soon filled the arena as the skater began her routine.

"Come on, Liz," Mike urged after a few moments. "You're being too hard on yourself."

"Mike, how would you feel if you messed up in a major way?" Liz countered. "I'm the head engineer! I'm supposed to be on top of things like that."

"But you didn't mess up," Mike protested. "*You* didn't change that tape!"

"Any idea how it happened?" Nancy asked.

Liz shook her head wearily. "Beats me. I had Elaine's tape all week. Her mother brought it up to me the day before the competition began. I ran a test on it that day, and it played just fine."

"Where do you keep the tapes?" George asked.

"Right here," Liz said, pointing to an open box on a counter beside her that held dozens of tapes. "That's where all the skaters' tapes are."

"Did anyone else have access to this room?" Nancy asked.

Liz nodded sadly. "This place was like Grand Central Station all week. Right, Mike? I mean with all the concern about the Optoboard, no one dreamed there'd be any problem with something like an audiotape."

"So anyone could have come in here and changed the tape?" George asked.

"That's right," Liz said, shaking her head. "I was in and out a lot and I never even thought of locking the door. I was too busy running around getting tapes from the trainers and running sound checks. Next time, I'm sealing this door like a mummy's tomb. Live and learn."

"Oh, no! Ann missed her triple Salchow," said

George, who was keeping one eye on the action on the ice.

The muscular skater pushed on, completing her routine, but when her scores were announced, they were low in both technique and artistry.

"Too bad," George said sympathetically. "But her routine wasn't very original. And missing that triple really hurt her."

Between skaters, Nancy and George said a quick goodbye to Mike and Liz. Then they hurried back to watch the rest of the program. Most impressive were Veronica Taylor and Trish O'Connell, who both wowed the crowd with their originality and inspired skating.

"Veronica really helped herself with that routine," Nancy remarked after she came off the ice. "With a good long program, she'll probably finish in the top four after all. Amazing, considering how badly she did in the compulsories."

"Amazing," George agreed. "She certainly recovered from that fall and the threatening letter pretty quickly." Frowning, she added, "Or maybe she just wants to show off for Kevin."

"Come on now, George," Nancy warned. "Don't let your feelings get the better of your good judgment."

"Anyway, she'll never catch up with Trish," George said. "That's a comforting thought. Trish is so brave, don't you think, Nan? Even with all the pressure on her, she's holding up like a true champion."

"You sound pretty sure she's not behind all the sabotage," Nancy observed, putting an arm around her friend's shoulders.

"Aren't you?" George asked.

Nancy shrugged. "I'm not sure what I'm sure of," she admitted. "I'll tell you what I'd like to do, though. I'd like to get down to the locker room before the skaters get out of their costumes. That way, we can check to see who might be missing a few sequins."

"Good idea," George agreed.

As Nancy and George approached the locker room, Nancy heard angry shouting coming from inside.

"What can be happening?" George asked, as Nancy pushed the door open.

Inside, Elaine Devery's mother was shouting at Trish O'Connell, who stood frozen at her locker, taking the angry words in. Nancy noticed that Trish's costume was a lovely shade of peach. It was decorated with many sequins, but none of them was blue. On the bench near her was an open tote bag.

"I don't know why you're being permitted to skate in this contest," Elaine's mother was saying. "It's an outrage!"

"Mom, this isn't helping," Elaine complained, gently leading her mother a few feet away and trying to calm her down.

Veronica was standing at a nearby locker hanging up a scarlet costume. "Don't let her get to you, Trish," Veronica advised.

Trish turned back and saw Nancy. "Hi," Trish greeted Nancy and George, a slight tremor in her voice.

"Trish, you were awe inspiring out there," Nancy said.

"Truly great," George agreed.

"Thanks," Trish said, trying to smile. It was clear from the expression on her face that Mrs. Devery's anger had dimmed her happiness about her performance.

"See?" George whispered to Nancy. "She's wearing peach."

"Are you talking to me?" Trish asked, punching in the digits of her locker combination.

"I was just saying how much I love your costume. The color is great," George replied.

"Thanks," Trish said, pulling the door open. She reached in and pulled out another costume. Nancy did a double take. The costume was festooned with hundreds of sequins—all blue, and all a perfect match for the ones Nancy had found during the blackout.

"This is what I'm wearing for my long program. Do you like it?" Trish asked, holding it up for their inspection. "I'm skating to *Rhapsody in Blue.*"

"It's lovely," Nancy said, reaching out and touching it gently.

"It's missing a few sequins," Trish pointed out. "I remember you found some in the hall, but they couldn't be from my outfit. It's been wrapped up until now. And besides, I wouldn't have any reason to wear it up on the press level."

Shrugging, Trish put her costume back inside the locker. Then she reached down and took a bottle of shampoo from the tote bag in front of her.

Across from them Mrs. Devery shook off her daughter's arm. "I just want to know why," she said, stepping closer to Trish. "Why did you steal Elaine's skates and ruin her tape? Are you really *that* jealous? Are you so afraid that Elaine will win?"

Mrs. Devery's face was flushed as she stepped even closer to the cowering Trish. "You even tried to kill Yoko Hamara. You're a sick person, Trish O'Connell! Sick and evil!"

"That's enough!" Veronica shouted, stepping in front of Elaine's mother. "Leave her alone!"

Sobbing, Trish slumped onto the bench, knocking against her tote bag as she did. The bag crashed to the floor, and the contents spilled out.

Nancy reached down to help pick things up. As she did, she spotted something that made her gasp. There, on the floor, was a small metal file. Nancy had a strong suspicion that she was looking at the tool that had been used to file the screws on Yoko Hamara's skate blades!

Chapter Eleven

"WHAT'S THAT?" Trish asked, staring at the file in Nancy's hand.

"Who cares? I'm getting out of here," Mrs. Devery muttered. She pushed past Nancy and George, calling over her shoulder, "Elaine, meet me upstairs when you're ready."

"Trish, this is your tote bag, isn't it?" Nancy asked, indicating the carrier.

"Yes, but that's not my file. I have no idea how that got in my bag," she said. "I certainly didn't put it there."

Veronica and Elaine leaned over and took a look. "Is that a nail file?" Veronica asked.

Elaine flushed bright red. "I know what that

is," she said. "It's what you file metal with. I happened to overhear Ms. Soren telling a police officer about some filed-down screws that were found on the ice right after Yoko's accident. You filed those screws down so they'd come loose, didn't you, Trish?"

Veronica stood up. "Listen, Elaine, I've known Trish for a long time," she said. "She'd never hurt anyone."

"Oh, get off it," Elaine scoffed, turning to Veronica. "You're just falling for her poor-little-me act. You're sticking up for her because she's like a sister to you. Well, she's no sister to me!"

Nancy studied each skater in turn. "We have to show this file to someone from the federation right now," she said.

"They'll throw me out of the competition for sure!" Trish moaned hopelessly.

"Which is the least she deserves," Ann Lasser whispered to Suzanne Jurgens, in a voice loud enough to be heard by them all. "They ought to throw her in jail!"

Tears welled up in Trish's eyes as she turned to the other skaters. "Since you're all so sure that I'm guilty, maybe I'll just quit."

"Fine with me," Elaine muttered.

"No, Trish," Nancy announced. "You're not quitting yet. Let's talk to Kathy Soren and see if she can tell you how to handle this."

Nancy walked over to the locker-room door and held it open. Hanging her head, Trish walked through.

Wordlessly, Nancy, George, and Trish made their way up the ramp to where the federation officials sat. Kathy Soren was putting on her jacket. Nancy guessed that she was getting ready to go to lunch.

"Ms. Soren, we found something else you should be aware of," Nancy said, handing her the metal file.

The former champion's face went white. "Where was it?" she asked.

Before Nancy could tell her, Trish stepped forward. "It was in my gym bag," she said. "But I didn't put it there. I swear I didn't."

Just then Mr. O'Connell stepped up to the group. "Hello there, everyone," he said. "Nancy, I need to talk with you—" He stopped when he saw their grim expressions. "Is something wrong?"

"Oh, Dad, I'm in really big trouble," Trish said in a whisper.

Mr. O'Connell was perplexed. He stroked his daughter's hair and glanced over at Ms. Soren. "What's this about?" he asked.

"Someone deliberately filed down the screws on Yoko Hamara's skates," she told him. "And a metal file was found in Trish's purse."

Gulping hard, Trish eyed the official and said, "I'm beginning to think I should drop out of the competition."

"Wait a minute, Trish," Nancy said cautiously. "If you haven't done anything wrong, there's no reason for you to do something so drastic."

"Nancy's right, Trish," George agreed. "Just because some people think you're guilty doesn't mean you have to drop out."

"Dropping out would be like admitting you're guilty," Mr. O'Connell insisted. "I can't let you do that, when I know you'd never do anything to harm anyone else."

Trish bit her lip and reconsidered. "I guess you're right," she finally agreed.

"Don't drop out, Trish," Veronica urged. "You've worked so hard to make it here. Besides, you're in first place now."

Trish let out a sigh. "But how can I continue? The federation won't want me in the contest if they think I'm hurting other skaters."

"That's true," Ms. Soren said, "but it's also possible that someone else is behind all this. I'll need to confer with Mr. Fleischman and some of the other ASF officials before we make any hard decisions about whether you should continue, but for now, you're still in."

"Okay," Trish said quietly.

Ms. Soren shook her head sadly. "I'm also going to tell the police about this right away."

"Oh, no!" Trish murmured. "I'm not going to be arrested, am I?"

Trish was interrupted by Ms. Soren's assistant, the woman with oversize glasses who had given out the passes the day before the competition began. "Excuse me, Kathy, but I know you'll want to hear this right away," she said. "I finally got through to the hospital. Yoko is conscious, and the doctors say she's going to be okay."

"Thank goodness," Ms. Soren said with a relieved sigh.

"Well, there's some good news for a change," Mr. O'Connell added.

"Will you all please excuse me?" Ms. Soren said. "I've got to make some calls." Holding on to the file, she left.

"I think I want to go back to the hotel," Trish said listlessly.

"I'll go with you," her father said. "We can get some lunch."

"I'm not hungry, Dad," Trish told him. "And I'd really like to be alone for a while."

"Want me to drive you?" he asked. But before she answered, he posed another question. "Why don't you take the car? I'll have lunch here at the arena," he said, fishing his keys from a pocket and handing them to her. "Drive carefully, honey."

Trish gave her father a peck on the cheek before she said goodbye to Nancy and George and turned to go.

"Have you had lunch yet?" Mr. O'Connell asked Nancy and George.

"No," Nancy answered.

"Then join me," he said. "I received some information this morning that I want to share with you."

"Okay," Nancy said. George nodded, and the three headed for the restaurant.

"Your photograph came in very handy," Mr. O'Connell said with a heavy sigh after they were seated and had ordered lunch. "The man's name is really Dieter Grunsbach, and he's one of the world's most notorious corporate spies. He's also got a prison record as long as your arm."

Nancy leaned back in the booth. "I didn't see him today," she said worriedly. "Do you think he's already out of the country?"

"I don't think so," Mr. O'Connell told them. "The minute I found out about all this, late last night, I contacted customs at both major airports in the area and they told me he hadn't left. Even if he drives to an airport in another city, customs will have been alerted to stop him. They'll search him with a fine-tooth comb. He'll never get out of the country with our chips."

"He must have another plan," Nancy speculated. "I'm sure he knew ahead of time he'd be carefully watched."

"That makes sense," George agreed. "I only wish we knew what it was."

"Me, too," Mr. O'Connell said.

Nancy paused as the waitress came with their sandwiches and sodas. "There's something else that's bothering me," she said, when the waitress had left. "How did Grunsbach know the exact location of the circuit board?"

"That's what I'd like to know," Mr. O'Connell said. "We tried to keep that information top secret. That's why we had a compartment constructed under the counter. Most people would assume the circuit board would be part of the main terminal."

"Let's try some logic," Nancy suggested. "Besides yourself and Rob, who knew where the circuit board was hidden?"

"Well," Mr. O'Connell said thoughtfully. "No one." For a moment his breath caught in his throat before he found his voice again. "No one, that is, except Trish."

Chapter Twelve

TRISH KNEW WHERE the Opto chip was located?" Nancy asked. "Are you sure?"

Mr. O'Connell let out a huge sigh. "Well, yes. I'm sure. It was the day we first arrived here. We checked into the hotel and came to the arena. That was when we first met you two, actually."

"I'm curious about something," George said. "If you and Veronica are from the same hometown, and such good friends, why didn't you travel here together?"

"I can answer that simply enough," Mr. O'Connell said, setting down his glass of water. "Trish and I didn't come here from home. We'd been in Ohio, visiting my mother."

Nancy nodded. "Mr. O'Connell, did Trish realize how big a secret the location of the circuit board was?" Nancy asked.

"Oh, yes," he replied without hesitation. "She knew how closely we had to protect that information."

"I see," said Nancy, trying to piece together what she'd just heard. "Mr. O'Connell, I need to ask a personal question. Do you and Trish get along well?"

Mr. O'Connell's eyebrows raised in surprise at the question. "Do Trish and I get along? Of course, we get along. Naturally, we have differences. All families do," he explained. "But we love each other very much."

His answer confirmed Nancy's gut feelings about Trish and her father. Trish didn't seem the type for deep resentments or destructive behavior. That was exactly why none of the clues pointing to Trish made sense.

With a weary sigh, Mr. O'Connell wiped his mouth and put down his napkin. "I was really looking forward to this contest to test the Optoboard in a real competition. I had no idea that things would turn out so badly, for me *and* for my daughter."

"I believe someone is setting Trish up," Nancy said. "Does she have any enemies that you know of?"

"Trish?" he asked, totally surprised. "Why, everyone loves Trish! Everyone who knows her, that is."

When the check arrived, Trish's father scooped it up. "This is on me," he said. "And now, if you'll excuse me, I want to go talk to Rob before the afternoon program begins. See you in the arena."

"He's really sweet," George said as Mr. O'Connell walked to the exit.

Nancy barely had heard George, though. Her attention was caught by a portly man who had just entered the restaurant. He was standing beside the cashier's desk, surveying the restaurant with his sharp eyes.

"George, look," Nancy said. "There's Gilbert Fleischman. Why is he standing there like that?"

The head judge's eyes seemed to light on a table at the far end of the room that was cut off from Nancy's view. She craned her neck but was unable to see what or who had caught his attention. "George, can you see who's sitting at the table behind that pillar?"

George turned her head in the direction Nancy asked. "Yes, I see," she said. "It's a group of reporters. I recognize Mary Joe Peck from the River Heights *Morning Record.* She's sitting with some woman with a terrible bleach job and heavy makeup."

"That's got to be Fran Higgins," Nancy said excitedly. "Remember? She's the one whose car Fleischman got into that night."

"Right. Now she's glancing over at the cashier," George said. "She's putting money on the table and getting up! Do you think she's meeting Fleischman?"

"Come on, George, we're leaving, too," Nancy said suddenly. "I want to see where they go."

"Fleischman is already gone," George said, looking toward the restaurant door.

"He's waiting for her, I'll bet," Nancy told her. "But why, George? Why are they sneaking around? Could he be working with Dieter Grunsbach? Could Fran Higgins be the female accomplice?"

Nancy didn't wait for an answer. The moment Fran Higgins reached the restaurant door, she got up from her chair. "Let's go," she said to George.

Outside the restaurant, Fleischman was nowhere to be seen. Fran Higgins strolled back in the direction of the main arena, but she soon turned off the main corridor into a small hallway. Holding back, Nancy waited for a moment before she peered around the corner.

Gilbert Fleischman was anxiously signaling the reporter to come to him. He was holding a door open for her and glancing around nervously. "Come in here," he said, breathless. "Hurry."

From around the corner, Nancy heard the door shut. When she looked again, no one was in the hall.

"They must have gone in that room," Nancy murmured. Moving closer, she saw that the door was plainly marked: Utility Closet.

George shot Nancy a quizzical look. "Isn't a

utility closet for brooms and cleaning equipment?" she whispered.

"Or secret meetings," Nancy put in.

"Let's listen," George suggested.

"Just what I was thinking," Nancy agreed, pressing her ear to the door.

"Yes, it's urgent, Frances," the head judge was saying. "It's been three years since we met, and two since I fell in love with you. I must know, right away—will you marry me?"

Nancy and George were both surprised.

From inside the small room, they heard Fran Higgins let out a hearty laugh. "Oh, honey, I thought you were never going to ask! The answer is yes, yes, yes!"

The utility room got very quiet after that and Nancy guessed that the prospective bride and groom were sharing a kiss. "Let's go, George," Nancy whispered, turning away from the door.

"I guess that clears up that little mystery," George said with a wry grin as she and Nancy made their way back to the arena to their seats for the pairs finals.

"It sure does," Nancy agreed. "But it doesn't clear up any other mysteries around this place."

As the arena was filling up again, the Optoboard put on a dazzling show, repeating highlights from the morning program. There was Trish, gliding to the pure sweet jazz she'd used in her short program. Her movements punctuated the music with dazzling leaps and sophisticated spins.

"Watching on the Optoboard is almost as good as being there in person," George remarked. Nancy had to agree.

Veronica Taylor's performance came next. In her scarlet-and-white outfit, she skated to a medley of movie themes. She skimmed the ice, boldly spinning and leaping, sure of herself and as graceful as a swan.

Next the board flashed the new standings in the women's competition. Trish O'Connell was still in the lead, by a wide margin now. Suzanne Jurgens was second, followed closely by Ann Lasser. Right behind them was young Terri Barton in fourth place. And in fifth, only a fraction of a point behind Terri, was Veronica Taylor. Elaine Devery was in sixth, in spite of all her problems. The rest trailed far behind. Yoko's name had been removed from the board.

"Veronica's back in contention now," Nancy said, summing up the standings. "She's really strong at free skating, too. I'll bet she makes it into the top four and goes on to the World Championships. Elaine, too. She's a great free skater, don't you think? Much stronger than Suzanne Jurgens or Ann Lasser."

"Yoko would have been in the lead," George said sadly. "She's better than any of them."

"True," Nancy agreed. "And the way things have been going, it's impossible to tell who else might be knocked out by more sabotage."

The announcer's voice came over the loudspeaker system, informing the audience that the pairs-skating finals would begin in ten minutes.

"What do we do next, Nan?" George asked. "I know you well enough to realize that we're not just going to sit here and watch the pairs skating."

Nancy grinned mischievously. "I want to talk with as many of the women skaters as we can," she said. "Everything points to Trish, but that's the problem—it's too neat and tidy. In my opinion, she's being set up."

"I agree," George said. "But who would do a thing like that?"

"That's what we've got to find out. We have to dig up some clues, and we've only got one more day."

"Where to first?" George wanted to know.

"There," Nancy said, pointing to the south end of the rink. Two rows of seats had been removed, and makeshift partitions had been set up to create cubicles where reporters could do interviews with the skaters. "I see some of the women skaters giving interviews."

"Hey," George said, getting up to follow Nancy. "Maybe I'll get to see Kevin. He mentioned that he had to interview Terri Barton."

Following George around the edge of the rink, Nancy soon came to the cubicles. George peeked around one of the partitions. When she popped her head back out, she said, "That was Suzanne Jurgens."

"There's the Worldwide Sports camera operator," Nancy said, pointing out a guy wheeling a camera toward the partitions.

"Last cubicle, Steve," a rink staff member told him.

"Aha," George said. She ran ahead of the cameraman to the last cubicle, with Nancy right behind her.

Nancy almost bumped into George because her friend froze in the cubicle entryway. Nancy couldn't believe her eyes when she saw what had made George stop short. Kevin and Veronica were standing inside the entrance. And they were kissing!

Chapter Thirteen

ALL OF A SUDDEN Kevin looked up and saw Nancy and George.

"G-George!" he stammered, clumsily breaking away from Veronica's embrace. "I, uh—um, I—"

Veronica gently stroked Kevin's cheek and patted him on the shoulder. "I can see you two need to be alone for a minute," she purred, moving to the doorway. "I'll be right out here, Kevin. Call me when you're ready to do our interview." With a wink and a wave, she made her way out past Nancy and George, not even glancing at them.

"I can explain," Kevin insisted as he wiped away the traces of red lipstick on his mouth.

George crossed her arms over her chest and glared at him.

"Oh?" she said icily.

"Well," Kevin began. "You see, we were waiting for the cameraman, and I was using the opportunity to learn more about Veronica, so the interview would go better. I learned quite a lot, actually."

"I'll bet you did," George said huffily.

"Then she started to flirt with me—right out of nowhere. And that's when you showed up."

"Yeah, right," George said sarcastically. "Wasn't that friendly of her!"

"Come on, George, you've got to believe me," Kevin insisted.

"I do?" George said.

"I have no idea why she kissed me. I certainly didn't do anything to encourage her."

George faced him squarely. "Kevin Davis," she began. "If you mean to tell me that you were just standing there, and all of a sudden Veronica Taylor started kissing you—well, you must think I'm totally dumb, which I am not!" With that, George stormed away.

Kevin watched her leave, then turned to Nancy. "I know it sounds farfetched and ridiculous, Nancy, but that's really what happened."

"Why would Veronica do something like that, Kevin?" she asked.

"I, uh, guess she just finds me very attractive or something," he said, running his hand nervously through his hair.

"On the other hand, she might just be looking for some extra publicity," Nancy suggested.

"Maybe," he agreed. Then he blew out a big breath. "But who cares about Veronica? It's George I'm crazy about!"

"You'd better go after her then," Nancy suggested.

"I know what I'll do," Kevin said, his face brightening. "I'll ask her to dinner at the Ridgefield Hotel. A lot of skaters are staying there. I heard the restaurant has great food and live music after ten."

Nancy grinned at him. "Sounds good to me," she said. As he took off, she called after him, "Good luck!"

"I feel dumb being here," Nancy protested as she and George walked into the Ridgefield Hotel dining room. "Why don't you have dinner alone with Kevin?"

"Absolutely not," George insisted. "I told him the only way I'd meet him was if you came, too. I said that from now on, he and I were just friends—and since we're all friends, we can all eat together."

Nancy sighed and rolled her blue eyes.

"I have my pride, you know," George continued. "If he expects me to believe that he had nothing to do with that kiss, he can forget it."

"I believe he was telling the truth, George," Nancy said gently. She took in the decor of the charming room, with its dark green table linens and small brass wall lamps.

"Oh, well," George said with a sigh. "I don't want to talk about it anymore today. I'll think about it tomorrow, when I'm calm and rational."

"There he is," Nancy said, pointing at a table where Kevin was sitting alone.

The second he laid eyes on George, he stood up and waved. "Over here," he called softly, so as not to disturb the other diners.

"You know, I wish Kevin weren't *quite* so good-looking," George said on their way over to join him. "Not that I'm going to let him get away with this. But it's hard to just *un*like someone you were crazy about only a few hours ago."

"Hi," Kevin said, concentrating on George, who let him pull out her chair before she sat down.

"This place is very nice," she said, but Nancy noticed the lack of enthusiasm in her voice.

"They have excellent food," Kevin said, settling into his own chair. "The seafood is fantastic."

After they consulted their menus and ordered, there was a lull in the conversation. Kevin didn't know what to say, and George was being purposely quiet.

"How have your interviews been going, Kevin?" Nancy asked to fill in the void. Instantly she wished she'd asked a different question. The memory of his interview with Veronica Taylor was all too fresh in everyone's mind.

Kevin didn't flinch, though. He seemed glad to have something—anything—to talk about. "Some of the girls have been a little tense because of all the weird stuff going on," he said. "Most of them are pretty angry at Trish, but they don't want to come right out and say it. But it changes the atmosphere when there's someone around whom nobody trusts."

"Do you feel that Trish is causing all the trouble?" Nancy asked him.

Kevin looked surprised. "Don't you? Doesn't everybody? Even the police are focusing on her, from what I hear from my producers."

"The evidence certainly seems stacked against her," Nancy said noncommittally.

"What did Veronica have to say?" George asked, a slight edge to her voice. "Anything interesting?"

Kevin nervously began tapping on the table. "Veronica—let's see," he said, attempting, unsuccessfully, to be casual. "Well, she's an interesting girl. A little sad, actually," he said.

"Oh?" George said coldly. "For instance?"

"Well, she's an orphan, you know. And she doesn't have a lot of money," Kevin replied. "The O'Connells have been very good to her. They've known her since she was a little girl. She and Trish belong to the same skating club."

"Does Veronica think Trish is sabotaging the contest?" Nancy asked.

"Oh, no," he said. "Definitely not. Veronica kept saying how sweet Trish is. I guess you never want to see anything bad in someone you like."

"I know what you mean," George said, glaring at Kevin.

Nancy tapped her fingers thoughtfully on the tablecloth. "I don't get it. How can Veronica afford a skating career if she doesn't have much money?" she asked. "Skating's an expensive sport."

"That it is," Kevin said, shaking his head sadly. "Veronica's always had a corporate sponsor—most good skaters do. They pay for training, costumes, ice time, travel—everything. Unfortunately for Veronica, the company that sponsored her was just sold to another corporation that doesn't believe in sponsoring athletes. She has to find another sponsor soon, or she won't be able to skate long enough to be in the Olympics next year—which has been her lifelong goal."

Suddenly George froze, staring at something across the room. "Speaking of the poor, dear girl," she said stiffly, "there she is."

Wearing a fluffy pink jacket and blue jeans, Veronica Taylor walked into the dining room. With her was Brian Adderly, Yoko's coach.

"Hi, Kevin," Veronica said, walking over to their table. "Hi, George and Nancy," she added. Brian walked up behind her and nodded to them.

"We were just at the hospital," Veronica went on. "Yoko's going to be okay. They're going to let her out of the hospital tomorrow. It was just a concussion. I'm so relieved!"

Brian Adderly was grinning widely. "She can't wait to get back on the ice."

Nancy was surprised. "Is she well enough to skate in the long program?"

Brian shook his head reluctantly. "Oh, no. She'll just be coming as a spectator. We're going to have to wait till next year to compete again. But Yoko's tough. She told me she's ready to get back to work as soon as possible, and her family agrees that it's a good idea."

"That's great," said George.

Nancy noted that Brian Adderly still thought of himself as Yoko's coach. Apparently, things had been patched up between them.

"Well, I don't want to interrupt your dinner," Veronica said, her eyes fixed on Kevin. "But I thought you'd want to know about Yoko."

Kevin glanced at the skater uneasily. "Oh, we did," he mumbled.

"Well, see you later. 'Bye, Kevin," Veronica cooed. Then she and Brian walked over to the hostess to be seated.

"That's it," George announced. "I'm leaving."

Kevin was shocked. "All I did was say hello," he said. "We don't even have our food yet!"

"I saw the way the two of you were looking at each other!" George said angrily.

"She was looking at me! I wasn't doing anything back!" Kevin protested.

George didn't say anything but simply got up from the table.

"Wait, George," Kevin pleaded. "Don't go."

Ignoring him, George asked Nancy, "Are you coming?"

"Yes," Nancy said, with an apologetic look at Kevin. "See you tomorrow, Kev."

Nancy followed George as she hurried from the dining room. "Ugh," George said, when they were safely out. "Did you see the way she was ogling him?"

"She does seem to have a crush on him," Nancy observed.

"Well, good for her," George said, fuming. "She can have him. Let's go home."

"Wait, George," Nancy said, grabbing her friend's arm. "I have a better idea. Trish and Veronica are rooming together. If Veronica is here, Trish may be alone in her room. Why don't we see if we can talk to her before we go home for the night? I'd like to see what she has to say."

George stared moodily at the restaurant door. "Okay," she finally said. "At least it should help me get my mind off Kevin."

Checking at the desk, Nancy and George found out that Veronica and Trish were in Room 724. They took an elevator to the seventh floor.

The girls followed the arrow under the sign

saying "Rooms 720–724." Just as they turned the first corner, Nancy stopped in her tracks and grabbed George by the arm.

There, furtively closing a door, was a slender man whom Nancy instantly recognized.

It was Dieter Grunsbach!

Chapter Fourteen

HER EYES RIVETED on the back of his head, Nancy motioned for George to stop. Questioning her with a look, George followed Nancy back around the corner and down the hall past the elevators. They ducked into the first hallway and waited.

Safely obscured from view, Nancy peeked out around the corner. Grunsbach walked quickly toward the elevator and pressed the Down button. A moment later he stepped into the elevator and disappeared.

"Come on, George," Nancy said. "Let's tail him!"

The two girls raced to the elevators, where Nancy pressed the Down button. When she scanned the floor indicator, Nancy grimaced.

Grunsbach's elevator was already at the first floor. The second elevator that Nancy was waiting for was stuck on the fourth floor.

"We're not going to make it before he leaves the hotel, George," Nancy said as both elevators stayed on their respective floors. "There's no sense even trying. Let's see which room he came out of."

Nancy and George went back to the door where they had just seen the corporate spy.

"Room seven twenty-four," George said, reading the gold numbers affixed to the door.

"That's Trish and Veronica's room," Nancy said, frowning. "I wonder what he was doing in there."

She fished in her purse and pulled out a flat case. "We'll soon find out," she added.

"Nancy! I don't believe you have your lockpick kit with you," said George, recognizing the familiar set.

Nancy only smiled as she used the delicate metal instrument to fiddle with the lock opening under the doorknob. A satisfied smile crossed her face. "Got it," she told George.

Inside the room, the overhead light was on. "Trish? Are you here?" Nancy called out.

There was no answer.

"George, do you realize what this means?"

Nancy asked, a sense of excitement rising in her. "Dieter Grunsbach has just linked one of these girls to the theft of the Opto chip!"

"But we know Veronica is downstairs," George pointed out. "That means he must have come here to meet Trish or leave a message for her."

"Let's not jump to any conclusions," Nancy warned. "Not yet. Right now I think we should just search for clues."

Nancy stepped inside the room, with George close behind her. A paperback book about the Olympics lay open on one of the beds. Veronica's name was written on the inside cover. "This must be Veronica's bed," George surmised as Nancy continued looking around.

On the long, low bureau between the beds were makeup bags, hot rollers, and hairbrushes.

"I don't see anything out of the ordinary," George said.

"I do," Nancy told her. "Check out the inside corner of the other bed, by the pillow." The beige bedspread was folded up slightly, unlike the one on the bed across from it.

"That must be Trish's bed," George said.

Nancy walked over and touched the covers lightly. She ran her fingers around the pillow and felt the tip of a business envelope.

"Aha!" Nancy said triumphantly, holding the envelope up for George to see.

"A message from Dieter Grunsbach?" George murmured.

"Probably," Nancy replied, examining the envelope. "We're in luck, too. It's not sealed."

She quickly pulled out the paper inside and unfolded it. "Hmm," she said, reading it over and then handing it to George.

" 'Sponsorship Arrangements,' " George read out loud in a puzzled voice. " 'The party of the first part agrees, upon receipt of certain items, to procure an arrangement for sponsorship with the party of the second part. This shall include reimbursement for any expenses occurred during procurement, allowing for total confidentiality of certain other actions on the part of the sponsor on behalf of the bearer.' "

George looked up from the letter, totally perplexed. "What in the world does it mean?"

"Either a lawyer wrote that, or else it's deliberately complicated so if anyone found it they wouldn't understand what it was about," Nancy said.

George's eyes lit up. "Nan, remember Kevin said Veronica needed a new sponsor?"

"Yes. I remember," Nancy said, her eyes narrowing. "On the other hand, that's Veronica's book on the table by the near bed. It looks as if it's under *Trish's* pillow."

Biting her lip, George tilted her head and thought about it. "How do we find out?" she asked.

"Well, for now, I think we put this back right where we found it," Nancy said, carefully replacing the letter inside the envelope and slipping it under the pillow.

"I'll check the closet for clues," George said, walking through the open door and disappearing.

"George?" Nancy called from the window, where she was searching behind the open drapes. "Find anything?"

George stepped out of the closet, appearing to be shocked. In her hands was a pastel-pink gift-wrapped box with a shimmery pearl ribbon. "I don't know whether to kill someone or cry!" George said, holding the gift up for Nancy to see. "Can you believe this?"

George's chin was trembling as she handed the gift to Nancy. Her wide brown eyes had filled with tears.

Nancy took the gift. There, on the little tag taped to the top, she read, " 'To Veronica, From K.D.' "

"K.D.!" George spat out. "Kevin Davis! That miserable, low-life, two-timing liar! Do you know he practically had me convinced that she forced that kiss on him?"

Nancy stared at the gaily wrapped box. Poor George. Nancy knew that if she ever found a gift to another girl marked with Ned Nickerson's initials, she'd feel very upset, too. "You'd better put this back where you found it, George," Nancy said.

George stared at the gift and back at Nancy, her eyes burning with curiosity. "Aren't we going to open it? I'm dying to know what that creep bought for his new girlfriend. I wonder if it's perfume. Maybe it's the same kind he gave me! I wouldn't put it past him."

"I think we should leave it alone, George," Nancy advised. "Where exactly did you find it?"

Still fuming, George waved the box in the air. "In the closet."

Before George could return the box, the door to the room swung open and Trish O'Connell walked in.

The skater looked from Nancy to George in confusion. "What's going on? Why are you in my room?"

George quickly put the wrapped box on the dresser. "Well, Trish, you see, w-we—" she stammered.

Slamming the door behind her, Trish marched over to the nearest bed and sat down. She raised her eyes and accused Nancy. "You're investigating me, aren't you! You think I've done all those awful things everyone else has decided I did, and you're in here snooping for proof!"

"That's not true, Trish," Nancy said. "The truth is, George and I *don't* believe that you did all those things. We think you're being set up. But here's the thing—we don't know by whom, and we don't know why. That's what we want to find out. And you've got to help us."

Nancy went over to the far bed and fished out the envelope she'd discovered. Holding it up for Trish to see, she said, "Let's start with this letter, Trish. Who's it from and what's it all about? It's time to lay all your cards on the table. *All* of them."

Chapter Fifteen

"LAY *MY* CARDS on the table? What cards?" Trish said wearily, slumping back against the pillow and squeezing her eyes shut. "This week has been one long nightmare," she said. "I feel like giving up. Maybe I should just confess to everything. I know that would make a lot of people happy."

"No one would be happy about it, Trish," George said softly from where she stood near the bureau. "But if you were responsible for what happened—"

Trish shook her head and reached for a tissue from the box on the night table. "I'm not responsible, George," she said, dabbing her eyes. "I guess I'm just feeling sorry for myself."

"Which is perfectly understandable," Nancy said gently. "But not very useful."

Trish straightened herself up and faced Nancy. "What's that letter you were showing me before?" she asked.

Nancy handed Trish the letter. Taking it in her slender hands, she read it and was very puzzled. "What is this? Some sort of sponsorship agreement?" she asked.

"You don't know anything about it?" Nancy asked, confused.

"Not a thing," Trish said, her face a blank. "Besides, you just pulled it out from under Ronnie's pillow."

Nancy raised her eyebrows. "That's funny," she said. "When we walked in and saw Veronica's book on your bed, we thought the letter must have been left for you."

"Oh, no," Trish said, managing a little smile. "This is my bed. Ronnie lent me her book the other day."

"So that letter *was* left under Veronica's pillow," Nancy said.

"I *knew* there was a reason I couldn't stand her," George muttered under her breath.

"Trish," Nancy said, "I think I know who's behind all the trouble. I also think that deep down you know who it is, too."

The skater's eyes filled with tears, and she bit her lip.

George let out a little, involuntary gasp. "Are you saying—"

Nancy met her friend's eyes squarely. "Let's go over everything. Someone put a paper clip on the ice, and Veronica fell."

"That could have been a total accident, Nancy," George cautioned.

"Possibly," Nancy agreed.

"The ASF is pretty careful about how the ice is maintained, George," Trish said, drawing her knees up and hugging them.

"Okay, let's go on," Nancy said. "Next, there was that threatening note that Veronica found in her sweater pocket."

Trish leaned forward with a little shiver. "Ronnie showed me that note. It was creepy. Doesn't it prove that someone was after her, too!"

Nancy shook her head. "Anyone can write a note in block letters—even the person the note's addressed to."

"But, Nancy," Trish insisted, "Veronica would never do something like that—just like I wouldn't."

"Maybe not," Nancy said noncommittally. "Then there were Elaine's skates, the ones that were found in your locker. Trish, when you got your locker combination, did you write it down?"

"I had to," Trish said. "Until I memorized it."

"And where did you keep the paper it was written on?" Nancy asked.

"In my wallet," Trish answered. "But I never left my wallet around for anyone to see. It was either on me or right here in the room."

"Right here in the room," George repeated, picking up on Nancy's thoughts. "Where Veronica could find it."

Nancy nodded. "How about your blue costume? Was that ever here in the room?" she probed.

Trish's face had grown pale. "Well, yes. Of course. This is where I kept it," she answered weakly.

"So Veronica had the opportunity to pluck a few sequins off the costume, to use as clues against you," Nancy pointed out.

"What you're saying is too awful, Nancy," Trish cried. "I hate hearing all this! Veronica's a good friend of mine! She wouldn't hurt me."

"Desperate people do desperate things, Trish," George said sadly. "You might have been the easiest person to pin the crimes on. You were close to her, so she had lots of chances to set you up."

Trish shut her eyes and shook her head.

"One last thing, Trish," Nancy went on gently. "Yoko had her blade screws filed down, and the file was found in your purse. Was that purse up here in the room, too?"

Trish hesitated and then nodded. "But I still can't believe what you're saying. You're trying to frame Ronnie, the same way someone tried to frame me!"

"Trish, I know this is hard on you, but let's stay with it a minute," Nancy told the skater. "The Opto circuitboard. Your dad told us that you knew where it was. Did you tell anyone else where it was located?"

Trish stared at Nancy. Then she covered her face in both hands and nodded her head. "I—I told my—my closest friend," she finally stammered.

"Veronica," Nancy said quietly.

The room was silent as Nancy, George, and Trish digested this last piece of information. Then Trish uncovered her face and went on, "My father told me not to tell anyone, and I wasn't going to," she said, gulping back tears. "Ronnie kept teasing me about making such a big deal about where some stupid computer chips were, and I thought I could trust her. Then, when the board was taken, I didn't say anything because Ronnie insisted that she didn't have anything to do with it. She told me she thought computers were boring."

Tears streamed down Trish's cheeks. "Oh, I—I just can't believe it!" she whispered. "It *has* to be her, doesn't it? I mean, otherwise, it's *me*, right?"

Nancy nodded gravely. "I'm pretty sure the man who stole the Opto chips left this note for someone in this room," she said.

Trish stared blankly down into her lap. "Oh, poor Yoko!" she whispered.

"No wonder Veronica was so relieved when

she got back from the hospital," George said. "She probably didn't mean for Yoko to get hurt."

"There's another problem," Nancy said. "A big one. We have to prove all this." She began pacing. "Everything I just said may sound good, but without proof, it's meaningless."

A breezy voice at the door interrupted them. "Hi, everybody!" said Veronica Taylor, sweeping into the room with a broad smile. "What's going on? Are we having a party?"

Nancy quickly put a finger to her lips to warn Trish not to say anything. "We just stopped by to say hello," Nancy said brightly. "But we're leaving now."

"I want to get to bed early," Trish said. "Big day tomorrow."

"By the way, you got a present," George told Veronica, pointing to the gift-wrapped box that she had set down on a bureau.

"I did?" Veronica said, surprised.

"Veronica, would you mind opening it while we're still here?" Nancy asked. "It looks so pretty, the way it's wrapped—and we'd love to know what it is."

Veronica quickly read the tag. " 'From K.D.' " She gave a nervous little giggle. Nancy could see George's jaw tighten, but George didn't say anything.

"I know Kevin would be embarrassed about it," Veronica said, her eyes darting nervously around the room. "He'd probably even deny it if you asked him."

"Open it," Nancy urged, handing her the gift.

"Oh, no," Veronica said, giggling nervously again. "I wouldn't want to rub it in," she added, flashing George a wicked look.

"I don't want to see it, anyway," George said stonily as she stared firmly down at the floor.

"But *I* do," Nancy insisted. "Please, Veronica. For *me*. After all, when you wanted me to come to the compulsories, I came, didn't I?"

"Oh, well," Veronica whispered. "If you insist." Slowly she untied the pink ribbon, then lifted the tape and removed the wrapping paper.

Opening a small white box inside, she pulled out a sparkling red and black belt made from beads and sequins.

"That's beautiful," George said. "Kevin certainly has good taste."

Veronica held the sequined belt to her slender waist and stared at her reflection in the mirror. "The best," she agreed with a wicked smile. "The absolute best."

Chapter Sixteen

FOR A MOMENT George could do nothing but stare at Veronica, her cheeks bright red. "I'm leaving," she said finally, and headed for the door.

"I guess I'll go, too," Nancy said.

"See you tomorrow," Trish said, getting up to close the door behind Nancy and George.

Out in the hall George stormed over to the elevator and jabbed at the Down button. "Oooh, I don't know who I'm madder at, him or her!" she fumed. "Did you see her face when she put on that belt? That superior little smirk? I could have strangled her right on the spot."

Nancy put a comforting arm around George's

shoulders. "Calm down. Remember, you wouldn't want to trade places with Veronica Taylor, anyway," she said. "Not with the kind of trouble she's going to be in."

"What do you mean, Nan?" George asked.

"I mean that people can't get away with the things she's done, no matter how talented they are," Nancy said.

"You said yourself that you don't have proof," George pointed out.

"True, not yet, George, but I have plenty of evidence," Nancy said. "One piece of proof—just me—and I'll be able to go to the police."

The elevator appeared and the girls got in. "Ugh. What a night," George moaned. "Nancy, is my mascara all runny?"

Nancy glanced at her friend's eyes and nodded.

"When we get to the lobby, I'll go wash it off," George said. "I hate wearing this stupid stuff, anyway. I'm not going to look like a raccoon just because of a jerk like Kevin Davis."

As soon as they got off the elevator, George headed for the ladies' room in the lobby. "I'll be out in a second," she said.

"I'll wait here," Nancy told her.

As George disappeared inside, Kevin appeared around a corner of the lobby. "Nancy!" he cried in surprise. "I thought you'd be back in River Heights. Where's George?"

"She's in there," Nancy told him, pointing to the ladies' room. "She was kind of upset when she saw the gift you sent to Veronica, Kevin."

"What gift?" Kevin asked. "I never got Veronica any gift."

Nancy blinked. Kevin seemed sincerely perplexed. "You didn't?"

"Why would I do something like that?" he asked indignantly. "You know, I'm convinced that Veronica's just using me to get extra media attention. It's fame she wants—not me."

Just then George stepped out of the ladies' room, clear eyed. "Hi, Kevin," she said, not meeting his gaze.

"George," Kevin said earnestly, "Nancy said that Veronica told you I gave her a gift or something? Well, I didn't—"

"Oh, please, Kevin," George said, "Let's not get into this right now, okay? All I really want to do is go home and get a good night's sleep."

With that she led Nancy out of the hotel by the elbow. "I had to get out of there, Nan," she said, sliding into Nancy's car. "The urge to clobber Kevin was getting the better of me."

"Then you did the right thing by leaving," Nancy told her.

As they drove home, George asked Nancy, "Why did you want to see what was in that box from Kevin?"

"Something about that gift was weird," Nancy told George. "First of all, if someone you had a crush on gave you a present, what would you do?"

"Rip it open right away."

"Me, too," Nancy agreed. "So why was it wrapped and sitting in her closet?"

"I don't know," George admitted.

"Secondly, Veronica was surprised to see it—or at least she pretended to be. Which would mean Kevin sneaked into her room and left it in her closet. That in itself is bizarre. Even if he could get into the room somehow, wouldn't he leave it out in plain sight?"

"I suppose so," said George.

"It occurred to me that maybe Veronica wrapped the present and addressed it to herself from Kevin. That's why I needed to see what was in it."

"But why would she do such a strange thing?" George asked.

"Good question," said Nancy. "To make you more jealous? To make Kevin look bad in some way? I have no idea."

"I'm not happy, George," Nancy said the next morning on the trip to the arena. "I still haven't come up with the one piece of proof to back up my suspicions and evidence about Veronica."

The two friends went over the details of the case again and again. "Everything points to Veronica and Dieter working together, and it all adds up, too," Nancy said. "But without that one bit of proof, she and Dieter might just get away with everything."

As Nancy pulled into the arena parking lot, George patted her shoulder comfortingly. "You'll come up with the proof, Nan," she said gently. "I know you will."

"Thanks, George," Nancy said as she got out of the car. "Are you going to watch the women's finals from the Worldwide booth?"

George acted shocked. "Are you kidding?" she cried. "I intend to stay far, far away from Kevin Davis from now on."

"I think you're being a little too hard on him, George," Nancy said as they stepped into the crowded lobby.

"Well, I don't," George replied, miffed.

"George, look!" Nancy said suddenly. "I think I see Mr. O'Connell going into the arena. I'd really like to fill him in on what we've come up with and see if he has any new information for us. Let's catch up to him."

Trish's father was swallowed up in the thousands of spectators who had come to see the crowning event of the American Skating Federation championships—the women's singles long program.

"There he is, George," Nancy said a moment later. She wove through the crowd after the Fiber-Op executive. Before they could reach him, an announcement came over the sound system.

"Ladies and gentlemen, we'd like to welcome a very special visitor to the arena. She's someone we expect to see on the ice next year. Will you please give a warm round of applause for Miss Yoko Hamara!"

"There she is," George said, pointing to Yoko,

who was sitting in the stands near the judges' station, waving to the cheering throng. A three-dimensional picture of the young skater waved from the Optoboard above.

"She looks great," George said happily, as she and Nancy joined in the cheering. "Next year, she'll sweep this contest, you'll see."

"I believe it," Nancy said.

When the cheering died down, she began searching for Mr. O'Connell again. "Too bad I lost him!" she groaned.

"I see him," George told her, pointing. "He's all the way on the other side of the arena, right under the Optoboard."

The two friends hurried over to Trish's father, but by the time they made it through the crowds, the long program was about to begin. The first skater announced was Trish O'Connell.

"We can't talk to him during Trish's performance," Nancy whispered to George.

Trish skated out of the holding area wearing the spectacular blue costume that she had shown Nancy and George and took her starting position. "Doesn't she look beautiful?" George murmured.

"She certainly does," Nancy agreed.

The stirring strains of *Rhapsody in Blue* soon filled the arena, and Trish took off, delivering as complex and skillful a program as Nancy had ever seen.

"Someday she'll be an Olympic gold medalist," George said softly as Trish leapt and spun, dazzling the audience with every new twist and turn. "I'd bet on it."

When the program was over, the audience roared its approval. Soon the judges held up the cards with their almost perfect scoring results. Mr. O'Connell, who was sitting just a couple of rows in front, leapt to his feet, cheering along with Nancy and George.

Next on the ice was Elaine Devery. As she skated to her starting position, Nancy moved closer to Mr. O'Connell and tapped him on the shoulder.

"I've got to talk to you," she said softly. "I learned a lot yesterday, and you should know about it." Without disturbing the other spectators, Mr. O'Connell rose and signaled Nancy to walk with him to one of the arena archways. George followed.

"We can talk here," he told the girls when they got to the concession area.

Nancy filled the Fiber-Op executive in on all of her ideas. "Dieter needed an accomplice," she said, "and it had to be someone who didn't have a police record. As for Veronica, she needed sponsorship, badly. Without it, her skating career was headed for a quick end. They made a perfect team."

Inside the arena, the crowd was cheering again. "That's for Elaine," George said.

Mr. O'Connell's face was obviously disappointed. "I can't tell you how shocked and upset I am to hear that you think Veronica is behind all this—especially that she may get away with it. I treated that girl like my own daughter. I mean, I can believe that an unscrupulous company like Krause-Deutschland would try to steal the Opto—"

"Excuse me, Mr. O'Connell," Nancy said, touching his arm. "What was that you just said?"

"I said how disappointed I am in Veronica," he began, but Nancy interrupted him.

"No," she said, "the name of the company?"

"Krause-Deutschland?" he asked.

"K.D.!" Nancy cried. "That's it! Come on, George. We've got to get hold of the police right away. In fact, see if you can find an officer and have him meet me at the holding area right away!"

Without a single question, George was off in search of the authorities.

"Come on," Nancy said, pulling on Mr. O'Connell's sleeve. "Veronica's not going to get away with anything. Neither is Dieter Grunsbach. Your stolen Opto chips are right inside this arena. I know exactly where, too!"

Nancy hurried back into the arena. When she got to the holding area, George was already approaching, with two police officers in tow. Quickly Nancy explained to them what was happening.

Out on the ice, Veronica Taylor was just taking her starting position. She was resplendent in a black costume with a sparkling red- and black-sequined belt.

"Should we grab her now?" one officer asked.

"No," Nancy answered calmly. "Let her have her last moments of glory. She won't be having any for a long, long time."

Veronica skated brilliantly. When her marks were posted, she had catapulted into second place, right behind Trish O'Connell. Roses fell at her feet as she waved to the cheering crowd, smiling and crying at the same time.

When she skated back into the holding area, Nancy, George, Mr. O'Connell, and the police were ready for her. The smile disappeared from Veronica's face when she realized they were waiting for her. "Is—Is something wrong?" she asked. Suddenly, her skates seemed unsteady beneath her feet, and her gaze kept shifting from Nancy to the police to Mr. O'Connell.

"How could you do it, Ronnie?" Mr. O'Connell asked her. "After we've been so close all these years."

"I—I don't know what you're talking about," Veronica stammered, backing up. There was no place for her to run except back onto the ice, and Terri Barton was already out there, skating.

"The belt, please," the policewoman said, extending her hand.

"The b-belt?" Veronica was breathing hard, and her eyes were darting desperately about.

"The belt, Veronica," Nancy repeated.

In a daze, Veronica unhooked the sequined belt and held it out to Nancy. Just as Nancy reached for it, Veronica seemed to remember what was at stake. "Why should I give it to you? You don't have a warrant! I don't have to give you a thing!" she spat out, yanking the belt back out of Nancy's reach.

As she did, the buckle smacked into the concrete wall. It came apart, and out fell a small circuit board that had been cleverly concealed inside.

"The Opto chips!" Mr. O'Connell cried as one officer scooped the circuit board up.

"Ronnie, why?" Mr. O'Connell asked, hurt and bewildered.

Veronica stared at him in stubborn silence for a moment. "I was sick of always being 'poor Ronnie,'" she finally snapped. "You—You live this charmed life. Maybe I wanted you and your darling daughter to know what it's like to suffer a little."

"And Yoko and Elaine?" Mr. O'Connell asked. "Did you want them to suffer, too?"

Veronica's whole body seemed to deflate. "I didn't mean to hurt anybody," she murmured. "I didn't want to hurt Yoko. Believe me, I never meant to—I needed a sponsor. You don't understand. I needed it." She couldn't go on. Sobbing, she sank to her knees.

"Come with us, Miss Taylor," said an officer, helping Veronica to her feet. "We can talk it all out at the police station. It'll be more private there."

Nancy and George watched them go, the two officers guiding Veronica between them, followed by Brett O'Connell, holding the precious circuit board in his hand. "We'd better go, too, George," Nancy said. "They'll need us to answer some questions."

Two hours later Nancy and George returned to the arena. They went straight down to the women's locker room. Trish was still there, in her street clothes now. She was being congratulated by the other skaters.

"I won, Nancy!" she cried as Nancy and George entered the room. "Can you believe it?"

"I believe it, all right," Nancy told her. "There was never any doubt in my mind."

"Who else is going to Berlin for the world championships?" George wanted to know.

"Elaine is," Trish told them. "She came in third, right behind Ronnie." Her expression suddenly darkened. "Oh, they told me the police took Ronnie away. Did they—"

"She had the Opto chips on her, Trish," George told her. "The circuit board was in the buckle of that belt. Her pal Dieter must have left it in the room when he dropped off her contract last night."

"He was just picked up at JFK Airport, in New York," Nancy added. "We found out at the police station."

"Wow," Trish breathed. "It's all so incredible. Was Dad with you?"

"Yes," Nancy said. "He's waiting for you outside."

"You know," Trish said, "I never wanted to admit it, even to myself, but I often had an uneasy feeling that Ronnie resented me. You know, because my family had money and my father was still alive."

Trish's face took on a sad, faraway look. "And I can't believe she would do that to Daddy, who's been totally kind to her."

"Hey," Nancy said gently. "This is your day. Don't let Veronica spoil it for you. You've been through enough."

Trish picked up her bag. "You're right," she said, the smile returning to her face. "Hey, you two, can you come to the ASF party at Harper's? It's for the skaters and their friends and family. I'd love for you to come—with Kevin, if you want."

She reached out to give Nancy and George a big hug. "Thanks for being there for me, you guys. I don't know what I would have done without you." Then, with a wave, she ran out to see her father.

"George," Nancy said, looking at a list of the final standings that was posted on the locker-room door. "Look who else is going to Berlin—Terri Barton. She came in fourth!"

"Ann Lasser is in fifth," George noted. "I guess that means she'll be going, too, since Veronica is sure to be disqualified."

Shaking her head, Nancy said, "Poor Veronica. I do feel sorry for her, don't you?"

"After the way she flirted with Kevin?" George shot back. "Not one bit!"

"Speaking of Kevin," Nancy said, "shouldn't we go upstairs and say hello?"

"I suppose so," George agreed. "I have been kind of rough on him."

"I told you something about that gift was phony," Nancy reminded her.

"I should have realized it, too," George said sheepishly. "Let's go upstairs and invite him to the ASF party."

"So you're not mad at him anymore?" Nancy asked, a wry smile crossing her face.

"Let's just say he was skating on some pretty thin ice there for a while," George said. "But now we're back on solid ground."

"That's great, George," Nancy said. "I knew it wasn't like you to drop a guy without at least giving him a second chance."

"Hey, Nan," George said with a wink, "I guess I just wasn't cut out to be an ice queen!"

Laughing, the two girls headed out of the locker room. "Wow! I'm glad we're going to this party," said George. "These last few days have been tense. I'm ready to have some fun! How about you?"

"Absolutely," Nancy agreed. "Absolutely, positively. Let's go!"

Nancy's next case:

Bess has just bought a cute yellow Camaro, and she and Nancy are off to a trendy riverfront restaurant to celebrate. But the sweet night out turns sour in a hurry. They return to the parking lot to find shards of broken window glass—and no Camaro. The River Heights car theft ring has struck again!

But what begins as a simple auto theft soon leads Nancy down a devious and dangerous detour. From the city's warehouse district to the local drag strip, she confronts a conspiracy that has already led to murder. As the shocking truth unfolds, Nancy realizes that the investigation—and her life—could spin out of control at any moment . . . in *HOT TRACKS,* Case #71 in the Nancy Drew Files™.